My Halloween

by Wendy Dale

MY HALLOWEEN ROMANCE

First edition. September 30, 2022.

ISBN: 979-8201737641

Written by Wendy Dalrymple.

Also by Wendy Dalrymple

Watch for more at https://www.wendydalrymple.com.

Chapter One

Tabitha Peterson stared up at the stain over her childhood bed as a creeping sense of dread settled in the pit of her stomach. The splotch was an ugly, rusty brown that crawled across the ceiling a little more each day, snaking its ominous fingers ever closer to her. Summer had been rainer than usual, and now that the seasons were changing, the true extent of the water damage overhead was becoming painfully clear. She frowned, knowing full well that her mother didn't have the money to fix the roof. Neither did she.

Tabby had only been back in her hometown of Fort Myers, FL — or Fort Misery, as the locals called it — for a month. In that short span of time, it had become obvious why she left in the first place. With each passing day, the walls of the tiny home she had so desperately wanted to escape from more than a decade ago closed in on her . Silencing a heart that yearned to wander was no easy task.

She had heard the term for her current situation before: delayed adulthood. Failure to launch. Tabby was well aware of the fact that she should have her own place and a steady, "grown-up" job by now, preferably one that didn't mind her multiple tattoos and technicolor hair. Then again, people always had a lot of ideas about what she "should" be doing. Up until that point, her carefree existence of hopping from state to state and following the breeze had worked out fine. But now, fearing that the very ceiling would collapse on her, Tabby realized that maybe it was time to settle down and create some real security for herself after all.

Phone in hand, Tabby scanned job postings like she always did as soon as her eyes opened each morning. Her current gig at the Liquid Café downtown was helping add to her savings account, but if she was going to get anywhere fast, Tabby needed to pick up more hours somewhere. She had done it all over the years: bartending, waitressing, festival work, pet sitting, and deliveries. With only a high school degree and a restless, intrepid spirit, her employment options had always been limited. But Tabby's job situation was a problem that she promised herself she would remedy ASAP. Now that she was well into her thirties, the allure and excitement of living without a plan was beginning to wear off. She needed the tools to be independent, and in her mind, an education was her ticket there.

Tabby's heart sank as she scrolled past all the jobs that she would be more than happy to apply for, if she only had the credentials. Event planner assistant. Office manager. Front end coordinator. All perfectly respectable, "grown-up" jobs. All requiring at least some amount of experience or college credits. She would be there soon enough. Her college entrance test was scheduled for next Monday, and her tutor said she was ready. Still, she had a hard time believing in herself. The idea that it would probably take her months more to find a job — and then more time after that to be able to afford a place of her own — was depressing.

Tabby was about to give up when a new posting caught her eye. She blinked and immediately tapped on the cracked screen of her phone, intrigued by the description and the location. The position was for seasonal work and would last no more than a month. Plus it was a third shift gig that would work with her schedule at the café. Not to mention that the pay was pretty good. It was no cushy office job with insurance and paid days off, but for now, this would definitely do.

Haunted Hike Actors Wanted, $15/hr, Must Bring Own Costume

Ty Treadwell's 28th Annual Halloween Hike is seeking new hair-raising talent for their infamous haunted hike! Thursday-Sunday, 7pm-1am from September 28-October 30. Must audition and sign a waiver. 18+. Previous experience preferred. Stop by Ty Treadwell's in person September 21 from noon to close to apply.

She blinked and checked the home screen on her phone for the date and time. It was a sign: 9:21 a.m. on 9/21. A cold shiver ran down her spine as she tapped her screen back to the ad again. The Haunted Hike at Ty Treadwell's Family Fun Park was one of her all-time favorite things when she was growing up. There wasn't a whole lot to do in her small south Florida town, but once a year, the arcade/batting cage/mini golf course/go-kart center hosted a truly epic haunted walk in the week leading up to Halloween. Did Tabby want to be a part of that? Hell yeah.

She swung her legs over the edge of her bed and stretched as a light knock sounded on her door.

"Come in," she yawned, arching her back and stretching like a cat.

"It's finished!"

Lucinda Peterson peeked in through the crack in the door, her glossy auburn bob bouncing. Tabby's mother beamed with pride as she held up a chunky crocheted sweater in black, orange, purple, and green acrylic yarn. The front patch pockets were in the shape of smiling jack-o'-lanterns, with the rest of the garment emblazoned in every possible Halloween motif, from bats and black cats to the silhouette of a witch riding over a full moon. To most people, the article of handmade clothing would seem like a monstrosity, but to Tabby, it was nothing short of amazing.

"I know Halloween is your favorite," Lucinda said. "If it fits, then I'll get started on your Thanksgiving one next."

"Mom, you didn't have to go through all this trouble," Tabby said, appreciating the green sequin detailing in the eyes of the black cat.

"Try it on!" her mother urged, holding the oversized cardigan in her direction. She hesitated as she continued to appraise the piece that her mother had been working on since she announced she was going to start community college. Tabby was no stranger to her mother's crochet creations. There were many photos from her childhood of her wearing various yarn dresses, hats and costumes. It was going to be ninety degrees that day, far from sweater weather, but she didn't want to spoil the moment.

"It's great," Tabby said, slipping into the sweater. The yarn was still brand new and soft against her bare arms. The kitsch Halloween topper was definitely not her style, more Bealls Outlet than Hot Topic, but she appreciated the gesture all the same.

"Do you have work today?" her mother asked. "You always say how the café gets so cold."

"Actually, I'm going to an interview today. Maybe I'll wear this, though."

"Oh yeah? Where at, hon? You know, Jo-Anne's is still hiring. I think the Spirit store is open for interviews too."

"Ty Treadwell's," Tabby said, shoving her hands in the jack-o'-lantern pockets. "They're looking for actors for the Haunted Hike. I figured it would be good work while I look for something more permanent."

"Okay then," Lucinda said, a hint of hesitation in her voice. She retreated toward the door, waving her finger in the air. "Just be careful. Remember how Erin Ashburn fell in a pothole and twisted her ankle? Those Haunted Hikes can be dangerous."

Tabby frowned and wrapped the sweater tighter. She couldn't bite her tongue any longer about the very obvious problem that her mother was ignoring.

"Mom," she said, letting out a deep whoosh of air. "Wait."

Her mother turned and glanced back at her with one hand on the door. Tabby pointed up at the tea-colored stain on the ceiling and gave her mother a sympathetic frown.

"You know we have to address this soon, right?"

Her mother's painted-on smile disappeared into a tight, thin line as her eyes flicked up to the ruined popcorn ceiling overhead. She returned to Tabby's gaze and gave a nod of acknowledgment.

"Is it okay if I call Uncle Steve and have him come out to look at it?" Tabby said.

"I'll call him myself," Lucinda said, her voice small and quiet.

"Thanks, Mom."

"I left you some breakfast in the microwave."

Tabby nodded as her mother exited the bedroom, the light in her eyes dimmed. She scanned her childhood bedroom and fought the urge to lay back down. It was nearly autumn, a time that usually left her refreshed and renewed, sharper than usual, like a fresh box of crayons or an unexpected cold snap. It was a time when change and magic still seemed possible in the world.

Inspired and now fully awake, Tabby slipped out of her new sweater, hoisted herself off the bed, and headed toward the bathroom on a mission. She needed a shower, breakfast and a big cup of coffee, and she didn't want to spend one more moment stuck inside her tiny box of a room. She had a casting call to answer, after all.

***

Ty Treadwell's Family Fun Park hadn't changed much since Tabby last laid eyes on it. The small entertainment center was owned and operated by Ty "The Man" Treadwell, a baseball legend and one of the only celebrities to come out of their small town. The combination arcade, mini golf course, and go-kart track was located off US-41, near a vast expanse of pine scrub forest. It had been a mecca to most kids in north Lee County for the better part of twenty years. Everyone had their birthday parties there in elementary school, and in middle school the Midnight Madness Haunted Hike was considered the epitome of cool. In high school, it was the place to go for dates or group hangouts with friends. However, from the faded sign to the torn batting cage netting, it was clear that the Fun Park had also seen better days. Now, as Tabby parked her mother's burgundy Chevy Lumina in the parking lot, a strange sensation flooded her senses — something bittersweet she didn't quite have a name for.

Tabby ran face-first into a wall of nostalgia as she stepped out into the parking lot and took in her old stomping grounds. It had been years since she had been there, but the moment she crossed the threshold to the main arcade room, everything came rushing back: the smell of popcorn and hot dogs, the black galaxy-print industrial carpeting, the cacophony of electronic MIDI video game sound effects, and flashing lights. All of it overwhelmed her senses and instantly, she was twelve again, spending her hard-earned money on claw machine games and Galaga.

Against her better fashion senses, Tabby had decided to top her usual black tee, jeans and Converse sneakers that day with her new Halloween cardigan. Even though fall in Florida was nowhere near cool enough for sweater weather, everywhere one went had AC that pumped out frigid air. The dark interior of Ty Treadwell's arcade lounge was no different, and Tabby rubbed her arms against the chill as she advanced deeper into her favorite childhood playground. She had spent many happy hours in that very room, racking up tickets for the prize booth by playing Skee-Ball, air hockey and the whack-a-gator game. The urge to plug some tokens into a machine tugged hard at her heart strings.

It was after noon on a Wednesday and the arcade was dismal and empty as she wound her way past games and snack tables. With school in session and tourist season over, Tabby wasn't surprised that only a few people milled around the space, trying their luck at the Vegas-style slot machines. Still, she had no idea where to sign up for the auditions, or whom to speak to for that matter. The information desk seemed like her best bet.

Decorated for the upcoming season with black and orange streamers, the information desk, which was also the prize counter, was situated at the far end of the main arcade. An older couple walked away with two golf clubs toward the door leading to the mini golf course as she approached. As they left, the sole employee in the building came into view. A stocky, stressed-out looking man in a red Ty Treadwell's polo shirt was hunched over the counter with his head in one hand and a phone in the other. He ran his fingers through his dark hair and then down through his full beard in frustration as he listened to whoever was on the other line. He leaned his forearm back on the counter and sighed into the phone as Tabby approached.

"Yeah, I got the papers. I'll look at them today if it's not too busy," he said, affecting a deep, gravelly voice that Tabby could sense all the way down to her toes. It was a voice that was oddly familiar and set off bells of recognition. Her lips drew into a curious grin as she struggled to place where she had heard it before.

"Okay. Yeah. Bye."

The man clicked off the phone and stood up from his bent-over position as Tabby leaned against the counter. His entire body language shifted as their eyes met and he broke into a wide, warm smile. The invisible wall of nostalgia came crashing down on her in waves of disbelief as she regarded the man who was once a boy she used to know. Her lower lip hung open for a moment before she could manage to say his name, a name that had been buried away in her heart for a long, long time.

"Donnie?" she gasped. "Is that really you?"

Chapter Two

Donnie Treadwell didn't think he would still be working at his uncle's Family Fun Park at the ripe old age of thirty-two. It was a sad fact that he had been standing behind that very counter for practically half his life. Sixteen years of booking birthday parties, selling go-kart tickets, answering phones and watching the world go by had made him, in the words of Jack Torrance, a "dull boy". It was all work and no play, and far removed from what he actually wanted to do with his life. Unfortunately for Donnie, Uncle Ty didn't trust anyone with the keys to the kingdom if they didn't have Treadwell as a last name. And if it weren't for the Haunted Hike, Donnie probably would have found an excuse to get out of working at the family business ages ago.

It was a slow, nothing-to-do Wednesday in September when Tabitha Peterson rolled into Ty Treadwell's life again. Tabby was someone that Donnie hadn't considered in a long time, though there was a period of his teen years when she was all he could think about. Sure, he was hoping that she would have shown up at their ten year reunion, but in all honesty, he didn't *really* expect to see her there. Tabby didn't even bother to go to their graduation all those years ago, and she was nowhere to be found on social media now. Tabby might as well have been a ghost.

Donnie knew it was her right away, of course, from the very moment that she walked in the door. Even with her shock of pink hair and a weird homemade-looking sweater, he easily recognized his old classmate from afar. Thankfully, the retired couple from Nashville took their time picking out mini golf putters so he could hide long enough to catch a proper glimpse. She had taken out her septum ring and was a little curvier in all the right places. Now, as she stared back at him with a smile of recognition on her face, Donnie felt himself at a loss for words. Why his former unrequited teen crush was back in town visiting his family business on that non-descript Wednesday was a mystery to him.

"Tabby?" he said, trying his best to act surprised.

"Hi," she laughed, the apples of her cheeks turning pink. "This is so strange. I mean, running into you like this."

"Yeah." He nodded. "I haven't seen you since... gosh, probably since graduation."

"Probably," she agreed, tucking a strand of electric pink hair behind her ear. "I just moved back to town a few weeks ago."

"Cool, cool," he said, wiping his damp palms against the top of his jeans. "What, er... what brings you into Ty Treadwell's?"

"I saw that there was a posting for the auditions today?" she said, biting her lower lip. "I always loved coming to the Haunted Hike as a kid. I thought I would give being part of the scare crew a try."

Donnie's mind blanked as his eyes focused on her perfect lips and the subtle cleft in her chin. Auditions? Today?

"Oh, right! The ad!" he said, slapping himself on the forehead. "Yes. That's me. Hold on."

Donnie fumbled under the counter for his clipboard where he planned to take down the names and numbers of potential new actors. So far, he had the usual crew working the event; it was going to be him as a swamp creature, his buddy Oliver working the chainless chainsaw, his cousin Melissa as a mummy, and her wife, Stefanie as a vampire. By his estimation, he needed at least twenty other workers to act as zombies, ghosts and other creatures of the night who jumped out from the woods at not-so-unsuspecting hikers. So far, Tabby was the first non-friend, non-family member to show up.

"So, you just need to put your name and phone number down there and sign this waiver," Donnie said, pushing a photocopied liability waiver across the counter. "Tryouts are here tomorrow at 8 p.m."

"Do I need to wear a costume?" Tabby asked, filling out her details on the paper. "Because I can totally do that."

"It's not required, but you can if you want," Donnie said, surprised. The pumpkins, bats and witch knitted into her sweater caught his attention. "You're a Halloween fan too, I see."

"Yes," Tabby said, looking down at her sweater. "I *live* for this time of year. My mother, on the other hand, lives for crochet."

Donnie's face warmed and he scratched at his beard as he shifted on his feet. Tabby Peterson was actually standing in front of him, signing up to try out for his Haunted Hike auditions. It was surreal. He wanted to say something, *anything* that sounded more normal and relaxed than he actually was at the moment.

"So, have you ever done this kind of thing before?" he tried.

Tabby winced and offered up a cringe. "Not exactly. But I did work as a birthday princess for a few years when I lived in Portland," she said, signing the waiver. "Now *that* was scary."

"I guess so," Donnie laughed. "What's a birthday princess?"

"Oh, you know," Tabby said. "I would dress up in a big, ridiculous dress and appear at little kids' parties. I just basically stood around for pictures, read them stories and pretended to be a princess."

"Well, that's acting then." He shrugged. "So you're okay with running around in the woods at night?"

"Definitely." She nodded. "I came here multiple times during Halloween when I was a kid. I know what to expect."

Donnie's face flushed even deeper beneath his mass of facial hair. Of *course* he remembered seeing Tabby there. He had been to every single special event at Ty Treadwell's since he was five years old, not to mention the fact that he played the part of the masked chainsaw killer at the end of the hike for well over a decade. Now was probably *not* the time to recall his many fond memories of gleefully chasing her and her friends through the darkened passage at the end of the trail.

Tabby passed back the signed waiver and looked up at him with big, wide eyes. "So, I'll come back here tomorrow at eight, then?"

Donnie blinked as she stared back up at him with her dark, endless irises. His mind went blank as his eyes trailed down the length of her neck to a vine tattoo creeping suggestively across her collarbone. Tomorrow? What was going on tomorrow?

"Oh! Right! The audition," he said, forcing his eyes back up to her own. "Yeah. Tomorrow at eight. For sure. It's going to take a couple of hours, so just be prepared to stay a while."

"No sweat," she said, shoving her hands in her pockets. "I'll see you then."

"Yep, I'll be here," he said, waving her off.

Donnie exhaled a long, deep breath as she turned back the way she came. He continued to watch as she opened the door to the outside and a blinding rectangle of light broke through the darkened game room. He glanced down at the stack of papers that his uncle had left for him and then up at the door again. Tabby Peterson. What were the odds?

As Donnie wrapped his mind around the long and tedious legal document that he was supposed to be studying, his thoughts drifted back to Tabby again. She continued to pop into his thoughts every time he pulled out the sign-up sheet that day as hopeful college students, local actors, and horror enthusiasts signed up for the gig. By the end of the day, sixty people stopped by to apply for tryouts, of which only about fifty or so agreed to the terms and signed the waiver. Still, the one person that he was looking forward to seeing the following day the most was right at the top of the list, her cursive handwriting adorably standing out against the other names.

That night, as their weekday closing time neared, Donnie surveyed the arcade and did his usual rounds of taking out the trash, vacuuming the common area and a general security check. Satisfied, he turned out the lights and locked up as he had done five nights a week for the last decade. If it weren't for the promise of a month-long reprieve in the Haunted Hike every year, Donnie didn't know if he could take being trapped working at the Family Fun Park much longer. Now, with his Uncle Ty's generous offer on the table, he was more caged in than ever.

Donnie started his truck and stared out into the vast forest surrounding the perimeter of the property. His floodlights shone on the entrance of the Haunted Hike near the mini golf course and, for a brief moment, something like a glimmer of hope settled into his heart. Constructing the spooky sets and special effects for the haunted walk was his one saving grace, his time to shine. Now, it was completely under his charge and he was determined to make it the best it could possibly be. Donnie pulled out of the parking lot that night thinking of new scare stations, decorations, unexpected, and scary themes he could add. He also considered the very real possibility of working alongside Tabby and what that might mean. Donnie continued to push away worries about Uncle Ty's offer and his uncertain future as he drove through the dark autumn evening toward home.

Chapter Three

"Order up! Spicy pumpkin spice latte for Sharon!"

Tabby placed the fragrant craft beverage served in a giant orange mug on the counter as a woman in a maple leaf-print t-shirt came to the counter. Tabby had been working hard on perfecting her latte art, something she had become fairly well-known for when she worked at the Mean Bean in Tacoma. She was rather proud of the pumpkin design she had crafted into the foam on top of the fall-flavored beverage. Unfortunately, Sharon of the leaf-print t-shirt didn't seem to notice. Tabby frowned and scoffed to herself.

"Some people don't appreciate art when they see it," she mumbled.

Her fellow barista Evan smirked back at her. "Some teenage girl asked me if I could do a portrait of her dog the other day. We do *not* get paid enough for that."

"You said it." Tabby sighed, checking the time on her phone. "I almost forgot. I gotta jet out of here early today, Ev. I have an audition tonight."

"Ooh, what for?" Evan asked, suddenly animated. "The Royal Palm Dinner Theater had an open call for Little Shop of Horrors last month and I missed it."

"Well, it's not a regular acting gig," she admitted. "It's for the Haunted Hike at Ty Treadwell's. I'm going to try out to be part of the scare crew."

"What's a haunted hike?"

"You know... it's like a haunted house, but in the woods."

"So you'll get paid to stumble through the trees and *scare* people?" Evan asked, hand to his heart in mock disdain.

"Yeah, but there's more to it," she explained. "You also have to be able to read the crowd and make sure you don't scare anyone too much. Don't want anyone to get hurt."

"Oof. No thank you, not for me. You go right ahead, though," he said, then paused. "Hey, what about your entrance exam? I thought you were going to take that soon?"

Tabby nodded. "Yeah, the test is tomorrow. I know I should probably be studying tonight, but being home is making me feel restless. I think auditioning for the Haunted Hike might be good for me."

"Hey, babe, whatever you need to do to get your head right is okay by me," Evan said, taking a dramatic slurp of black coffee. He glared at her over the rim of his cup.

"What?" she said, playfully throwing a dish towel at him.

"Are you sure there isn't something else going on?" he said, catching the dish towel. "You've been singing and dancing around here all day. I've never seen you so... *happy*."

Tabby flushed and folded her arms across her chest. "Ugh. It's like you're a psychic or something."

"Not a psychic. Just a Virgo," Evan said, settling in. "Spill it."

"Okay, okay," Tabby said, covering her hot face with the palm of her hands. "The auditions are being run by this guy I knew from school."

"Ooh, an old crush," Evan said, raising an eyebrow. "Cute?"

Tabby rolled her eyes and blushed deeper as she recalled Donnie's impressive frame and full beard, his soft, laughing eyes the color of amber, and shy, boyish expressions.

"Yeah."

"Well, what're you waiting for?" Evan said, putting down his coffee cup. "Get the heck outta here."

Tabby undid the strings on her apron and kissed Evan on the cheek. "Thanks. You're sure you're good?"

"Yeah. Terrance will be here in ten minutes. Things are always dead between six and eight anyway."

"You're an angel," Tabby said, clocking out before Evan had a chance to change his mind. She waved over her shoulder and checked the time again. If the bus was running on schedule she would barely make it in time to get home, take a quick shower and beg her mother to use the car again that night. She would be at the mercy of borrowing her mother's car for another week, or at least until she could get her next paycheck, and then she would have enough to get a clunker. The Haunted Hike gig would help to expedite her plans for the future and get her mobile even quicker.

As the LeeTran bus came into view, Tabby picked up her pace and sprinted down the sidewalk. A brisk breeze blew through First Street as her sneakers pounded cement, and for the first time in a long time, a bubble of excitement rose inside her chest. As the last waning rays of sunlight dipped behind the Fort Myers skyline, the hair on her arms stood on end. A sour-sweet fragrance filled the air.

Change is on its way, Tabby promised herself as she got on the city bus. She slid into the seat, plugged in her earbuds and closed her eyes. She imagined Christmas in her own apartment with her own little tree next to a purple velvet couch. She imagined getting a job with benefits and paid time off. Maybe she would be able to get a cat, a black one. As the bus bumped along toward US-41, Tabby continued to remind herself of all the things that she was working so hard for. Her personal and financial goals. An independent future. A brand new life. All of that and more was waiting for her on the other side of fall.

***

"What color do you want for your next sweater, burnt sienna or mustard seed?"

Tabby tucked her t-shirt into the waistband of her jeans, her hair still damp from the shower. Lucinda was holding a skein of yarn in each hand, one brown and one yellow. Tabby danced in place a little and propped her hands on her hips. She didn't have time to discuss crochet with her mother at that moment.

"I don't know... the yellow, I guess? Sorry mom, I've gotta go. The audition starts in fifteen minutes."

"What time will you be back?" Lucinda said, the corners of her mouth turned down. "I was hoping we could watch *Unsolved Mysteries* together."

"I'll probably be late," Tabby said, offering an apologetic half-smile. She hated the look of disappointment on her mother's face. If Lucinda had her way, they would spend every night in front of the TV with a crochet hook in one hand and the remote in the other. Tabby was always too restless for that.

"I'm off on Monday," she offered. "We can hang out then."

Her mother nodded. "Be safe," she said, picking at the yellow yarn.

"I will."

Tabby grabbed the keys from the bowl on the kitchen island as her mother dove into her next project. Another pang of guilt settled into her chest as the screen door slammed behind her. With every passing year, her mom was becoming more reserved and closed off. Lucinda had always been more like a big sister to her, a side-effect from being a teen mom, no doubt. Tabby and her mother couldn't be more different, but when it came down to it, they were all each other had. Lucinda never said it outright, but Tabby suspected that her mother felt abandoned by her need to stretch her wings and explore the world. Even though she couldn't change the past, she was home now, and Tabby was going to keep her head down and work hard to make up for lost time.

The tires of the old Buick crunched along the long, unpaved drive leading toward US-41 as Tabby scanned the radio stations for something to listen to. She smiled as she found 99x and an alt-rock song from her teen years blasted over the speakers. Time really had come full circle: here she was, borrowing her mom's car to go to the Haunted Hike on a school night. Classic.

During the short five minute drive to the Family Fun Park, Tabby wondered what exactly the Haunted Hike auditions would entail. Would she be judged on the way she stumbled around and moaned? Would she have to do her best zombie impersonation? She was game for anything, but as she turned into the Ty Treadwell's parking lot, Tabby realized that getting the job might not be as easy as she anticipated. Dozens of cars were already lined up in the overflowing lot, and she had to crane her neck to try and find a parking spot. Tired of circling the lot, Tabby created a parking spot for herself in the grass next to the batting cages. She did one last hair and makeup check in the visor mirror and sprinted toward the floodlights and crowd near the treeline of the property.

With every step she took in the dark toward the Haunted Hike entrance, Tabby could sense her anticipation building. The memory of the first year that she was allowed to go with Tiffany Shepherd and Gia Santos without parents came rushing back as she approached. They had all worn their best new "fancy" t-shirts and jeans that night and clung to each other in the dark, shrieking every time a masked actor lurched out at them through the trees. Every rush of adrenaline brought Tabby to life, and now that undeniable sensation of excitement and Halloween nostalgia was returning. Only now she would have the opportunity to be on the other side of the scares, creating a fun and spooky atmosphere for a whole new generation of kids.

As Tabby approached the congregation of seated Haunted Hike hopefuls, a broad-shouldered man in a baseball cap came into view. She settled into a folding chair on the edge of the crowd and smiled as she recognized Donnie, now out of his uniform and casually dressed in a black tee, a plaid shirt rolled at the sleeves, and jeans. He had changed quite a bit from the wiry, smart-alecky kid from their graduating class. Donnie had been cute back then, if not a little entitled and full of himself. But now? Now he looked like a big, huggable bear in flannel and denim. It was a transformation that Tabby approved of way more than she would have liked to admit to herself.

"Thanks everyone for coming out tonight," he said, his deep voice booming out over the crowd. "The auditions are pretty simple and straightforward. We'll have security stationed all throughout the hiking path to watch out and make sure that everyone is being safe. What we need you to be able to do is show that you can handle being at your station, on your feet and in the dark for an extended period of time. We rotate actors and give you on-the-clock, fifteen minute breaks throughout the night so you can go to the bathroom or get a drink, but be aware that this gig is not for the faint of heart. Even at night, it's hot out there and we want to make sure our guests and employees don't get hurt."

Tabby grinned as Donnie continued to hold court over the scores of hopeful Haunted Hike actors. He answered questions about payroll, costumes, and accessibility for guests and employees with special needs before Tabby raised her hand. Donnie turned and locked eyes with her through the crowd, and for a moment his serious expression broke. A smile crept into the corner of his mouth as he pointed to her.

"What's the theme for this year's Haunted Hike?" she asked. As dozens of masculine heads whipped around to look at her, Tabby discovered that she was in a minority.

"Glad you asked," Donnie said, his smile fully on display now. "The theme is classic monsters. We already have a Wolf Man, a Bride of Frankenstein and a few others. If you need some help coming up with costume ideas then I'll be more than happy to help with that."

Tabby wiggled in her chair, itching to get started now more than ever. She knew *exactly* what kind of costume she would wear if she was chosen. She was already mentally planning her trip to Jo-Anne's fabric store with her mother as Donnie clapped his hands and started again.

"Hey, so are we going to get paid for tonight?" a boy who couldn't have been older than eighteen asked out of turn.

"Yes," Donnie said, turning to his voice. "If you make it through the one hour trial, we'll pay you for your time. Even if you decide this isn't for you or you don't get hired, you *will* get paid for the work you do tonight."

The crowd murmured among themselves and shifted in their seats. It occurred to Tabby as she noted the disdain oozing from the other hopefuls that most of this information could have been spelled out online somewhere before bringing everyone to the middle of a field on a Thursday night. She admittedly never organized an event like this herself, but it was clear that there were a few kinks in the hiring process that could be ironed out.

"So, if everyone is ready to give this a try, let's head to the trail," he said, his gaze connecting again with Tabby's. She couldn't really tell through the dark, but his features appeared more pinched and strained than usual as the crowd rose and murmured among themselves. Two people took off toward the parking lot but the rest of the crowd shuffled in a wave toward the entrance to the Haunted Hike. She steeled herself for the task ahead as her sneakers crunched through the field of dry autumn grass and leaves toward a darkened path. In all of her various odd jobs, Tabby had never been so psyched as she was at that moment to find a gig that married all of her interests and fit her so well. And the fact that Donnie Treadwell was there too? Well, that was a frighteningly delicious added bonus.

Chapter Four

Donnie didn't know what the *hell* he was doing. He was an idea man. An artist. He wanted to come up with concepts and do the work to make his vision a reality. He didn't want to manage or organize *anything*. Yet, here he was trying his best to onboard a group of nearly fifty prospective employees to undertake a very specific, possibly dangerous job, and by all accounts, he was failing. Miserably. Worst of all, he was failing in front of Tabitha Peterson.

Tabby had been the only person in the entire group of hopeful actors to ask about the theme for the Haunted Hike that year. It was a theme that he was particularly proud of, too, one that he had been working on since January. As a long-time lover of horror films and all things spooky, it was a great pleasure of his to be able to mold this year's Haunted Hike in his absolute vision. In the past, Uncle Ty had insisted that their themes be more cohesive and consistent with popular trends, like zombies or clowns. While those tried and true themes worked and still drew in crowds, Donnie had always wanted to take the Haunted Hike a step further and really make it special. Now, as the responsibility for the success of this year's event was put squarely on his shoulders, the pressure was on to make it the best that it could possibly be. If only he knew how.

"Okay everyone, we've got stations marked every fifty feet through the trail," he called out. "Just pick a partner and double up. Our team will begin walking through the trails once everyone is in place. It's going to be your job to jump out and try to scare us. But remember, no touching, no screaming and no profanity. Oh! And keep a distance of six feet at all times."

More grumbles sounded from the crowd behind him as they entered the first stage of the trail, causing Donnie's shoulders to tighten. He could tell that his auditions weren't off to a great start, and now as prospective actors wandered aimlessly on the Haunted

Hike path, he sensed that things weren't going to get much better. His embarrassment grew as annoyed scare actor auditionees complained to one another, struggling to find hiding spots along the trail. The Haunted Hike was the same as it was every year and spanned a quarter of a mile in length, winding through the pine scrub forest behind the mini golf course and ending at the batting cages by the parking lot. There were twenty scare stations in total, each marked with reflective signs that would be removed during the actual event. The hike itself only took about ten minutes to get through at an intentionally slow pace, but getting the prospective Haunted Hike actors into place seemed like it would take even longer.

"Hey man, you doin' okay?"

The walkie talkie at Donnie's hip blipped as his cousin's voice buzzed through in a haze of static. Melissa was already waiting at the far end of the hiking trail to help direct auditionees and get them into place. If anyone else understood the stress of putting on a Ty Treadwell's event, it was her.

"I'm drownin', Mel," he said, looking over his shoulder. "I should have hired someone to help us organize things."

"Don't sweat it," she said, her voice crackling over the receiver. "I'll walk toward your direction and start to herd some folks into place. We'll get through this."

"I owe you a beer," he said.

"Make that two beers," she laughed. "Over and out."

Donnie let out a deep sigh as more and more actors milled about looking for a place to get into position. It was then that he spied a familiar shock of pink hair, glowing through the dark of night.

"I think I see a spot down there," Tabby said, directing a group of teenagers toward the lagoon scare station. The "lagoon" was actually an old above ground swimming pool that he had sunk in the ground for the swamp creature scene. It was simple but effective and one of Donnie's favorite new additions that year.

Tabby offered up a smile of recognition as he neared. Donnie's heart nearly skipped a beat as she floated toward him, beaming in the dark. Even back in high school, Tabitha Peterson had been intimidatingly confident and cool, and from the look of it, that hadn't changed. Donnie, on the other hand, had lost his teenage cockiness somewhere along the way. He smiled back at her, squared his shoulders and attempted to look large, in charge and not at all terrified as she approached.

"Hey Donnie," she said, shoving her hands in her back pockets. "I was just gonna go hang out over at the cemetery."

"That's a good station." He nodded, his chest tight. "Lots of big tombstones and trees to hide behind."

"Hey, I had an idea for a costume that I wanted to run by you later," she said. "If I make it past the tryouts, that is."

"Yeah!" Donnie said, more enthusiastically than he intended to. He cleared his throat and continued. "I mean, sure. Do you have plans tonight after tryouts?"

"Nope," she said, her eyes sparkling up at him. Donnie reminded himself to exhale, then inhale.

Don't be a coward, Donnie, he reminded himself. *Ask her!*

"I'm going down to the Indigo Room with my cousin after tryouts to get a few beers after we're done. You wanna come along?"

"The Indigo. Classic." She nodded, smiling up at him. "Haven't been there since I needed to use a fake ID."

"Ha ha," Donnie said, the words more of a nervous chuckle than a laugh. He was striking out left and right all night. If Tabby said no, he could add the disappointment to his rotating pile of failures.

"I'll be there," she said, shooting him a double thumbs-up. "Okay, I'm gonna go duck behind a headstone. Wish me luck."

"Good luck."

He blinked. The world titled ever so slightly as Tabby and her mass of glowing hair disappeared down the trail. The walkie at his hip beeped and Donnie was snapped back to reality as Melissa's voice floated into the night.

"Everyone is in position at this end."

"That's a roger," Donnie replied. "Heading your way."

With the hiking path cleared of confused actors and everyone in their places, Donnie started down the path that he knew so well. It was a warm late September evening, but Donnie was already feeling the Halloween spirit as a full moon waxed through the trees. The smell of decaying slash pine needles filled the air as new fallen oak leaves crunched underfoot in the dark. By this time next week, the Haunted Hike would be filled with Halloween ambience, including artificial fog, eerie flashing lights and piped-in music. For now, his lonely walk was serenaded by the sound of the last summer cicadas and crickets to guide him through the woods.

The first scare station was of course the lagoon, his favorite area in the entire Haunted Hike. He would be hanging up his chainless chainsaw that year and opt for a custom swamp creature costume instead. The makeshift pool was far too dangerous to ask any actor to work in, and besides, the Creature from the Black Lagoon was one of his all-time favorite underrated monsters. Two teens jumped out from behind a tree as he passed and managed to keep the appropriate distance. He gave them a thumbs-up and continued down the path.

Next was the abandoned drive-in theater station, which was basically a couple of old, rusted cars and a hanging bed sheet for a movie screen. Donnie had the idea to play old black-and-white films on a loop throughout the Haunted Hike, but he hadn't quite figured out how to set up the projector yet. A man and a woman jumped out from behind the cars as he passed, also keeping the appropriate distance. So far, the tryouts were going pretty well.

After the drive-in movie theater was, of course, the cemetery, one of the biggest areas of the haunted hike. Uncle Ty had ordered dozens of custom-made headstones some twenty years ago with gag names on them like "ULE B. SORRY" and "I TOLD YOU I WAS SICK". Donnie's heart beat a little faster as he approached the cemetery, not because he was anticipating a jump scare, but because of who might be there waiting for him. His intentions were laser focused on finding Tabby and her warm, bright smile as he edged along down the path. His thoughts were clouded by her high cheekbones and mass of soft, candy-colored hair. He was so caught up in his daydreams that he didn't even realize that he was walking right into a trap of his own making.

"Ahhh!"

Donnie clutched at his chest as a hand reached out for him from behind a headstone that read "NOAH SCAPE." A tinkling laugh filled the air as a head full of highlighter pink hair came into view. Tabby stood to her full height, her hands covering a smile as Donnie caught his breath.

"Tabby!" he exclaimed, smiling back at her. "Oh man, you actually got me."

A loud grunting sound jerked him out of his trance as an inhuman growl came up from behind. Tabby shrieked and hit the ground as an enormous, dark form zoomed past her into the path. Donnie's fear immediately turned to anger as he recognized a giant of a man from the audition floor. He stood there in the path, hulking, snorting and pounding at his chest like a maniac.

"Hey man! Not cool!" Donnie said, bending over to help Tabby to her feet. "I specifically said no contact! That means with other actors, too."

The snorting, chest-thumping actor stopped and dropped his hands to his side. The man blocking their way on the path easily outweighed Tabby by a hundred pounds and several inches. His overacting and rough actions could have really hurt her or a potential guest. Suddenly, Donnie wasn't mad; he was *pissed*.

"I thought we were supposed to act *scary*," the man said.

"That wasn't scary," Donnie said, pulling Tabby to her feet. "That was just you being a jerk. Sorry man, but I don't think you're going to work out."

The man snorted again and kicked at the ground. "Nobody wants to work at your rinky dink haunted house operation anyway," he grumbled.

Donnie and Tabby stared at the man's back as he sauntered off. They locked eyes again and shared expressions of disbelief. Donnie gave her an apologetic look and was about to speak when Tabby yelled back at the man.

"It's a Haunted *Hike*, dumbass!"

Donnie laughed and shook his head as the man disappeared from sight. It had been a long time since he had to dismiss an actor for being too rough, but Tabby didn't seem too phased. He didn't want anyone to get roughed up on the hiking path, least of all his employees.

"Sorry about that," he said. "Are you good?"

"Yeah, I'm fine," she said, examining the palm of her hand. "Bro types like that can get overly excited at these things sometimes."

"That's exactly why we do the auditions," he said. "If you're okay, I'm gonna get back on the trail."

"Yep, I'll get back to my grave now." She laughed.

Donnie turned and waved, his blood pressure still spiked as another actor caught him by surprise near the zombie woods. All through the rest of the Haunted Hike tryouts, Donnie struggled to retain his focus, thinking only of how his mishandling of the auditions could have hurt Tabby or someone else. He wasn't cut out to organize a big event like this, but it wasn't like he had a choice. If Donnie wanted the Haunted Hike to live on at Ty Treadwell's, he had to take matters into his own hands. And maybe, just maybe, if the event was a success this year, he wouldn't feel like such a failure.

As the 9 p.m. hour rolled near, Donnie concluded the Haunted Hike auditions and thanked everyone that came out for their time.

All of the actors except for the graveyard jerk were invited to work the event, and as everyone retreated to the parking lot, Donnie had a chilling realization. He still had no idea how payroll worked, or who any of the new people were at tryouts. Melissa always took care of that part, but this was her last year working the event. If he didn't get some help and get it fast, this could be the final Haunted Hike at Ty Treadwell's Family Fun Park.

Chapter Five

Tabby checked the time on her phone as she sipped on a pumpkin cider later that night, the scraped skin on the palm of her hand throbbing like a heartbeat. It was almost 10 p.m., her fall flavored beverage was nearly half gone, and Donnie was nowhere to be seen. The cold glass was soothing against the cut on her hand and she was happy for the glass of liquid relief, but in truth, she was ready to go home. After a full day of working at the café followed by auditions, Tabby was bone tired. She had been waiting at the bar at the Indigo Room for nearly twenty minutes, and was almost about to give up and head home when a deep voice sounded in her ear.

"You're hired."

Tabby nearly snorted cider through her nose as she turned to see Donnie and two vaguely familiar women belly up to the bar.

"Hi," she said. "I was beginning to think you ditched me."

"No way," he said, smiling down at her warmly. "Besides, I believe I owe you a drink."

"You just want to avoid a lawsuit," she joked.

"You got me there," Donnie laughed, scooting into the seat next to her. He gave the bartender a nod of recognition and held up four fingers. "We'll take a round of whatever she's having."

"Thanks," Tabby said, waving to the two women on the opposite side of the bar.

"Do you remember my cousin, Melissa?" he said.

Tabby pursed her lips and knitted her eyebrows together as she reached back into the dusty recesses of her memory. She got a better look at the woman who had been busily taking down names and handing out cash to all of the new Haunted Hike actors an hour before.

"Melissa *Ridinger*? I didn't know you two were cousins!"

Melissa smiled and waved back. "Uncle Ty is my mom's brother," she said, slapping a hearty hand on Donnie's shoulder. "Donnie is my *little* cousin."

"Only by a month," he corrected, motioning to the other woman. "This is Melissa's wife, Stefanie. They work the Haunted Hike with me."

"Nice to meet you," Tabby said. "Gosh, I guess I forgot what a small town Fort Myers is."

"Tabby just moved back to town," Donnie explained, nodding to Melissa and Stefanie.

"You escaped!" Melissa said. "Why on Earth would you ever come back?"

"My mom," Tabby shrugged. "And... I'm going to go back to school soon."

"Good for you," Stefanie cut in, elbowing Melissa. "There's *nothing* wrong with moving back home."

"Yeah, yeah. You're right," Melissa said. "Stefanie wants to move back home to North Carolina and start an organic produce farm."

"A girl can dream." Stefanie shrugged.

Tabby took a sip of her drink, now re-energized by the company. She was an extrovert to the extreme and loved meeting new people, especially when they matched her energy.

"So what's stopping you from moving?" she asked.

Melissa and Stefanie shared a look and then glared back at Donnie.

"What?" Donnie said, taking a deep sip of his drink. He made a face as he gulped the sweet drink down. "Oh that's different. I thought that would be beer."

"No way, it's almost Halloween. That calls for fall-flavored beverages all the time," Tabby insisted. Her eyes darted back to Melissa and Stefanie who were still eyeing daggers at him.

"What's that look for?"

Donnie sighed and made a face. "I've been putting off some paperwork. It's a family thing," he said. "Uncle Ty is leaving the Fun Park to us."

Tabby's mouth opened wide as she involuntarily reached out and gave him a playful shove. "You're going to *own* Ty Treadwell's? Get outta here!"

"It's not set in stone yet," he said, holding up his hands. "I've still got some kinks to work out."

"That's so great," Tabby said, raising her glass. "Cheers to that."

"I guess," Donnie said.

Tabby's eyes flicked back to Melissa and Stephanie as they rose from their seats with their ciders in hand. A very loud country rap song blared over the speakers, causing Donnie to make a face. Melissa leaned in and yelled over the music.

"We're gonna go over there and see if we can talk the DJ into playing something else," she shouted, waving. "Tabby, good to see you again. Good job out there tonight."

"Thanks, Mel," Tabby shouted back. She gulped her cider, conscious of the fact that now she and Donnie were alone together at the bar. After a few more sips of her new drink and a long, music-filled pause, she spoke again.

"So, the Haunted Hike opens next week?"

"What?" Donnie shouted.

Tabby leaned in closer, her lips only inches from his ear. Even then, over the loud electronic western song, she had to speak loudly. He was so close now that her nose filled with his scent, a combination of laundry detergent, musk, and... candy?

"The Haunted Hike," she said, her eyes focused on the curve of his ear. "It starts next week?"

"Yeah," Donnie nodded, turning his head to her. His cider-scented breath was hot on her cheek as he huddled close to speak to her over the noise.

"We'll have a couple more trial runs on Tuesday and Wednesday. Paid time, of course. Then on Thursday we go live."

"I'm really excited," Tabby said, her hand cupped to his ear. "When I was a kid I looked forward to the Haunted Hike all year."

"Me too," Donnie said. His eyes met hers as the Indigo Room continued to pulse all around them. She was exhausted, but so grateful for a night on the town in a familiar place with familiar faces. Being so close to Donnie was comforting and exciting all at once, and the urge to reach out and feel the texture of his flannel shirt was strong.

The music was lowered a few decibels as Tabby turned her head toward the DJ booth to see Melissa and Stefanie were chatting with the DJ. Tabby stared back at Donnie and realized that they were practically face-to-face. She leaned back in her seat and took a long, deep sip of her drink as Donnie cleared his throat.

"So, um… you were going to tell me about your costume idea?" he said, changing the subject.

"Hmm?" Tabby said, taking another deep sip of pumpkin cider. "Oh, yes! So the drive-in movie area gave me an idea. Did you know that Hitchock movie *The Birds*?"

"Yeah," he nodded, his mouth forming a curious grin. "Go on."

"Well, I was thinking," she said, biting her lower lip. "What if you run that scene where Tippi Hendren gets swarmed by the birds on the bed sheet screen on loop? Then I can run out from between the cars dressed like her, but covered in fake birds? Am I making any sense?"

Donnie's curious grin broke into a wide smile as he finished off his drink.

"You know, I've been trying to figure out what to do with the drive-in movie area," he said. "I think that's a great idea."

"Really?" she said, excitedly grabbing his shoulder. "Oh, you won't be disappointed. It's going to be so cool."

Tabby's eyes trailed down to her hand. She was letting her touch linger too long. She pulled it away and rested her hands in her lap, trying hard to pull back. It had been a long time since she had been out, connecting with someone, and she was aware of the fact that she had the tendency to get a little too touchy and overeager. Still, Donnie didn't seem to mind the attention.

"What's your favorite Hitchcock film?"

"Oh that's easy," she said. "*Rebecca*. What's yours?"

"*Rear Window*," he said. "Everyone always says *Psycho*, and it's a classic for sure, but not his best."

"Well, Hitchcock is a little overrated anyway," Tabby said, suddenly animated again. Talking old horror movies and anything spooky in particular got her blood pumping.

"So, you're a Halloween expert *and* a classic film buff too," he said, shaking his head. "That's it. You're perfect."

Tabby's face burned. She was usually good at taking compliments, but somehow, Donnie's flattery hit her hard.

"If I was so perfect, I wouldn't be living with my mom again," she sighed. "I also wouldn't just now be starting college. All of my old friends are married with a couple of kids and a mortgage by now."

Donnie nodded and took out his wallet. He thumbed through the leather billfold, located two twenties and gave them to the bartender.

"We all have a different path, I guess. I mean, right? That's what I'm trying to tell myself, anyway," he said. "Taking the traditional route isn't for everyone."

Tabby blinked and smiled at Donnie as he rose from his bar stool.

"I wish I could be that kind to myself," she said. "Speaking of, I should be going. I've got an exam in the morning."

"Oh?" Donnie said, following her to the door. "What for?"

"Edison College. I'm going to try and get a business degree. Eventually."

She glanced down at her phone as the spider web-cracked screen glowed back at her. It was already after eleven as she rose from her seat toward the exit. Donnie told the bartender to keep the change. Tabby opened the door leading out to First Street as a crisp, moonlit evening greeted her. She was grateful for the cool air as it hit her hot cheeks. Donnie followed close behind. Now without the busy, noisy bar scene to fill the space between them, the silence of downtown was deafening and heavy with expectation.

"Hey, so I'm also working the opening shift at Liquid Café for now," she said, pointing to the darkened café down the road. "If you stop in, I'll whip you up a spicy pumpkin coffee that'll make every day feel like Halloween."

Donnie glanced down the street and laughed. "I just might do that," he said.

Tabby chewed on her lower lip and gazed back up at Donnie, his eyes hidden in shadow from the street light overhead. She was all warm and soft as she stood next to him on the sidewalk, like her insides were filled with caramel or marshmallow. A fleeting sensation overwhelmed her as she stood there melting in front of him. She didn't want to go home yet. Tabby could be very happy standing on that street corner and talking to Donnie forever about everything and nothing at all. However, with her exam to think about in the morning, it was long past time to say goodnight.

"Well, I suppose I'll be seeing you on Tuesday for practice, then," he sighed, shoving his hands into his pockets.

Tabby nodded and spied her mother's car parked on the side of the road.

"Yep. I'm gonna get to work on my costume this weekend. I'm pretty sure they have fake black birds at the Dollar Tree."

"Nice," Donnie said. "I can't wait to see it."

Tabby rubbed at the sore spot on the palm of her hand and gazed up at Donnie again.

"Thanks for stepping in with that guy on the trail," she said. "It feels good to know that you look out for your workers like that."

"He was completely out of line," Donnie said, his face suddenly dead serious. "I don't know. I think maybe I'm not cut out to handle an event like this."

Tabby shook her head. "You'll get it. You've got the passion for it and at least you're focused on treating people right," she said. "That's more than I can say for plenty of other places I've worked at."

Donnie's expression softened again. "Thanks," he said. "That means a lot."

Tabby waited for another minute, not sure what she was hoping for. After another moment of awkward silence passed, she glanced back at her car and then at Donnie again.

"Okay, well, goodnight then," she said.

"Night."

Tabby clutched the car keys in her hand, still feeling like something had been left unfinished. Her head spun as she opened up the car door, but it wasn't from pumpkin flavored cider. All of her local friends had either moved away or were too busy with their lives to bother making time for her. It was heady and wonderful all at once to have made a friend, albeit an unexpected one.

"Hey Donnie," she called out over First Avenue.

He turned on his heels and glanced back at her with one hand on the club door.

"You didn't tell me what costume you'll be wearing for the Haunted Hike!"

Even in the dark, Tabby could tell that he was smiling as he opened the Indigo Room door.

"It's a surprise!" he shouted back.

Tabby shook her head and waved to him as she slid behind the wheel of the car. She turned over the engine as 99x filled the cab with more alt-rock music. She smiled to herself as she pulled out onto First Avenue toward home, as the events of the past twenty-four hours replayed in her mind.

A surprise, she smiled to herself. *It surely is.*

Chapter Six

"All right, sign there, and there and... done."

Donnie scooped up the thick stack of papers and tapped them against the prize counter before handing them to Melissa. She took the documents and thumbed through them, making certain that he had signed near all of the lawyer's sticky notes. It was nearly closing time at Ty Treadwell's Family Fun Park, and the last day that Donnie had to finish signing the legal documents for his cousin. A huge psychological weight lifted from his shoulder as she slipped her copy of the property agreement into a folder and gave him a reassuring smile.

"I guess that's it, then," she said. "You still feel good about this?"

Donnie shook his head. "No. But I don't think I'll ever feel like I actually know what I'm doing with this place."

"You'll be fine," Melissa assured him. "I'll help you find someone to take my place and train you to do payroll before we move. Piece of cake."

"Yeah," Donnie said, rolling his eyes. "You didn't say what *kind* of cake though."

Melissa laughed through her nose and gave him a look. "You gotta give yourself more credit," she said. "You're more capable than you think."

"I'm just stuck in my own head, I guess," Donnie said. "By the time Uncle Ty was my age, he had already been named MVP, broken three world records *and* opened this place up. All I've done is manage a Family Fun Park."

"Comparison is the thief of joy," Melissa said, patting him on the back. "You have a different kind of gift, Donnie. Now's your chance to make the most of it."

Donnie shrugged. "We'll see," he said. "How am I gonna run this place without you and Stef?"

Melissa sighed and gave him a half-smile, half-frown. "You'll figure out a way. We all do," she said, leaning over the countertop. "Excited about the Haunted Hike rehearsals tonight?"

"Yep," Donnie said, bending down behind the counter. "I finalized the swamp creature mask this weekend. I hope the latex will last."

He stood upright and placed the green, scaly headpiece on the counter. With red glass eyes, realistic-looking fins and sharp shark-like teeth, even self-deprecating Donnie could admit to himself that his mask turned out pretty good.

"Dang, Donnie!" Melissa gasped. "You're gonna scare the pants off people in that thing."

"Well, that's the point," he said. "I know what you mean, though. Thanks."

"What's your girlfriend's costume gonna be?" Melissa asked, her eyes twinkling.

Donnie clammed up as his face grew hot and red. He frowned and returned his mask to its paper bag.

"Oh, come on. You can talk to me," Melissa urged. "Tabby is totally your type. I could see that coming from a mile away."

"She's also technically my *employee*," Donnie said. "I knew going out for drinks was a mistake."

"Only for seasonal work," Melissa reasoned. "Look, I'm glad you're being a gentleman about it and all. I'm just joking around."

"Don't worry. I wasn't even on her radar back in high school," Donnie said. "She probably won't see me as anything other than a friend at best."

"There you go again," Melissa said, shaking her head. "You know, taking ownership of this place is going to be good for your self-esteem, I think."

"We'll see about that."

Before Melissa could continue her lecture, a couple dressed as zombies ambled through the front door, followed by a woman in a blood-splattered prom dress. Donnie smiled as a killer clown followed them into the arcade followed by a corpse bride.

"Well, looks like it's time to slip into my Frankenstein getup," Melissa said. "See you out on the trail."

"Yep," he nodded. "See ya."

Donnie closed the register for the night and went to grab his costume bag when he spotted Tabby. His eyes fluttered in slow motion as a blonde dressed in a green form-fitting vintage-style dress stepped through the arcade double doors. Her hairstyle and makeup were from another era, her stockings were ripped and bloodied and she stomped across the galaxy print floor as if it were a red carpet. For a split second, he was completely enchanted until the black birds tacked to her shoulders and encircling her head caught his attention. Donnie let out an involuntary laugh as Tabby approached and performed a small curtsy.

"What do you think?" she asked, twirling. "Too many birds?"

"Wow. You *nailed* it!" Donnie said. "You look exactly like the movie."

"Glad you approve, Mr. Hitchcock," she said, leaning on the glass case. "Were you able to get the projector to work?"

"Yep," he said. "You're all set for your drive-in debut."

"Awesome," she said, raising her eyebrows. "Will you tell me what your costume is going to be now?"

Donnie smirked. "Nope. It's a surprise," he said. "You'll find out soon enough."

"*Fine*," she said, in mock disdain. "I'll see you out there then."

"Yep," Donnie said, swallowing hard. His heart hammered wildly in his chest as she walked away, the glossy black birds on her costume bouncing with every step.

Keep it together, dude, he told himself. He closed his eyes and inhaled a deep lungful of air before releasing it like a valve. He clutched his bag and headed to the restroom to change, suddenly regretting his choice of costume.

Too late now, he thought as he shoved the door to the men's restroom. *It's showtime.*

***

Donnie stood in knee-deep water as an eerie fog billowed through the trees in ghostly wisps. In the distance, a man screamed as the buzz of a chainsaw crackled and ripped through the night air. Somewhere nearby, organ music wafted through the breeze, followed by a succession of thunderclaps and clanking chains. The stomping feet of teenagers sounded at the head of the trail and he knew it was time to make his move. They shrieked with glee as he splashed through the man-made swamp with arms extended, stopping his chase shy of six feet from their heels.

Everything was falling into place for the Haunted Hike practice that night. By all accounts, Donnie was pleased. His swamp creature costume was holding up, his actors were getting in the groove at their respective stations, and all of his special effects were working as they should. By 10 p.m., Donnie was confident that things were going to go smoothly for their opening day and called it a wrap. Still in his swamp creature getup, he meandered down the trail to the drive-in movie theater station, his pulse picking up speed again.

As he expected, a classic black and white horror movie scene looped on the makeshift drive-in screen at the scare station next to his. The actress onscreen ran as a flock of black birds terrorized her, and Donnie observed with vested interest as Tabby burst from behind the screen, shrieking and waving her hands in the air. The group of teenagers that Donnie had hired to test out the Haunted Hike didn't even see her coming and let out a blood-curdling scream as she tore through the set. Donnie chuckled to himself from under his mask as he approached, arms extended.

"Boo."

Tabby turned and covered her mouth with a muffled yelp. Her eyes narrowed as she positioned her hands and body into a self-defense stance.

Donnie slid his mask down. "Hey, it's just me!"

"Donnie Treadwell!" she yelled, dropping her hands to her sides. "You scared the life out of me!"

"I think I'm the one that should be scared," Donnie said, holding up his hands. "Looks like you were ready to kick my ass."

"I've lived in a bunch of sketchy places over the years," she said, adjusting her wig. "A girl's gotta be ready to defend herself at any time."

"Noted," he said.

"Wow," she said, her voice breathy. "Did you really make that costume yourself? It's terrifying."

"Yeah. Special effects are kind of my hobby."

Donnie scratched the bridge of his nose as the sound of the chainless chainsaw buzzed through the air.

"I think we're good for practice tonight," he said. "I was going to head down the path and let everyone know they can go home."

"Cool," she said. "I'm starving. Have you eaten yet?"

Donnie's stomach growled at the mention of food. His dinner had been popcorn from the concession stand six hours ago. Heck yeah he was hungry.

"Uh, I could eat," he said. "Why?"

"My co-worker at the Liquid Café also works as a server at The Edison. He's been asking me to come in and check it out," Tabby said. "Wanna go get a burger?"

Donnie's elevated pulse kicked into overdrive. He had already made the mistake of going out with a potential employee for a beer. Now she was proposing dinner. His heart and his stomach said yes, but his head was screaming no.

"It's cool if you can't," she said, picking at one of the birds on her shoulder. "I can pick up some drive-thru on the way home."

"Yes," Donnie blurted out, clenching his fist at his side. "I mean, sure. I just need to wrap things up here first."

"Cool," she said. "I'll meet you down there then."

"Sounds good," Donnie said. "Give me about thirty minutes?"

"It's a plan," she said, turning on her heel. "I'll save you a seat!"

Tabby took off down the path as the birds surrounding her head on wires comically bobbed along with her. Donnie clutched his mask in his hand and broke into a light jog, more eager now than ever to shut down the Haunted Hike for the night. As he hurried toward the cemetery in anticipation of a horde of zombies, all he could think about was a double bacon cheeseburger with a side of fries, and a girl covered from head to toe in birds.

Chapter Seven

Tabby tapped her feet and wiggled in her seat as she pretended to study The Edison's menu for the tenth time. She had been waiting for Donnie for almost thirty minutes as an overwhelming sense of déjà vu slowly set in. She was overeager, as one former friend stated. *Too friendly.* Her energy and enthusiasm to become BFFs with everyone she met had a tendency to make some people feel bombarded. It was a personality trait that Tabby had worked on over the years, but she was starting to suspect that she was failing when it came to her new boss. Only when the nagging voice of her self-doubt made itself known did a pair of broad shoulders in a black tee and jeans fill the entryway of the downtown diner, causing the synapses in her brain to misfire.

Back in school, Donnie was a lanky, class clown type of guy. He was cocky and sure of himself, riding high on the notoriety of being Ty Treadwell's nephew. She laughed under her breath at the jokes he would tell in class and giggled along with everyone else when he would kid around in the lunchroom. But they ran in different circles, never really managing to connect. She and Donnie shared a common history, but somehow still managed to pass by each other like two ships at sea. Now he was sailing directly toward her, and had grown into a very different kind of man than she would have ever expected.

"Sorry I'm a little late. One of the zombie kids twisted his ankle on a cypress knee," Donnie said, taking a seat. He was all smiles as he slid into the chair across from her.

"What?" she asked, taking a sip of water. One of the faux black birds pinned to her shoulder pecked her cheek as she raised her arm.

"I should have stayed in costume too, I guess," he said, eyeing the menu.

Tabby patted her head. The blonde wig was still secure. She shrugged. "I didn't think to bring a change of clothes. Besides, I really like this dress. Got it for a steal at Flowers to Fifties."

Tabby's eyes adjusted in the dim restaurant light as she made out the faded screen printing on Donnie's shirt. Her lower lip fell open into a wide oval of disbelief.

"Is that a *Monster Squad* t-shirt?"

Donnie looked up at her over his menu with wide eyes and then down at his chest. He plucked at the tee with his pointer finger and thumb and threw her a surprised smile.

"Yeah, I got it off of eBay a million years ago. It's one of my all-time favorite movies."

"Mine too," Tabby said, her mouth still agape. "I played out my VHS copy until it broke."

"Hey, did you know that the wolf man in that movie was played by—"

"Uncle Rico! From *Napoleon Dynamite*!" Tabby said, her face completely flushed.

"Yes!" Donnie laughed. "Oh my gosh, people look at me sideways whenever I start to rave about that movie."

"I know. It's so underrated," Tabby said, clearing her throat. She had been famished during the Haunted Hike practice. Suddenly, her hunger had almost completely disappeared. Tabby glanced around the interior of the restaurant and shook her head.

"My grandpa would have been nuts about this place," Tabby said. "He was a big fan of the Edison winter estate. He loved researching local history."

"Yeah. It's a shame that our town is mostly known for being Thomas Edison's vacation home," Donnie said. "Of course, *I* always try to tell people that our town's real claim to fame is that Romero filmed *Day of the Dead* here."

"Exactly!" Tabby smirked.

As they both chatted about their favorite films, Tabby's fellow Liquid Café barista, Evan, appeared from thin air like an apparition. He hovered over their table with a notepad in hand and a Cheshire cat grin spread across his face. Tabby made a face as he launched into his act.

"Ready to order?" he asked, giving her a wink.

"I'll have the Bright Idea burger," Tabby said, handing him the menu.

"Excellent choice," Evan said. "And for you?"

"I'll do the same," Donnie said, handing over the menu.

"Donnie, this is my friend and coworker, Evan," Tabby said, rolling her eyes.

"Nice to meet you," Evan said. "Tabby has told me so much about you."

Tabby's eyes grew wide and her lips pursed into a thin line as Evan lingered a moment too long. He broke away from Donnie's awkward gaze and gave Tabby a devilish grin.

"I'll just get this ticket in," Evan said, and turned heel.

Donnie sipped his water as Tabby shot daggers in Evan's back. She was beginning to regret bringing Donnie to The Edison in the first place.

"I wonder why the Edison Home only gets decorated for Christmas," Donnie said. "Did you ever go on tours there as a kid?"

"Oh yeah," Tabby said, grateful for the change in conversation topic. "Every year."

"It would be the perfect setting for a haunted house," Donnie mused.

"Yeah," Tabby said. "Does Ty Treadwell's ever do a Christmas-themed hike?"

Donnie blinked and stared up at her with a strange sort of expression.

"No," he said. "Why?"

Tabby shrugged. "It seems like a good opportunity," she said. "You could do one for each season. A Christmas hike with Santa at the end. Maybe a romantic Valentine's Day hike. I dunno."

Donnie rubbed the back of his neck. "Yeah, I never really thought of that. I've always been so focused on designing the Haunted Hike and the whole Halloween aesthetic."

"So you really designed all of those sets?" Tabby asked. "Did you go to school for that or anything?"

"No," Donnie said. "I learned from a lot of trial and error. I love doing it. I get to work with my hands and be creative. I don't know if I would be as good at designing sets that aren't scary though."

"You don't know until you try," Tabby reasoned.

"Speaking of school," Donnie said, leaning forward. "Didn't you have your college entrance exams or something recently?"

Tabby frowned and nodded. "Yeah, but I don't think I did so hot. I won't get my scores until next week."

"I only did one semester at Edison after high school," he shrugged. "It wasn't for me. I wish that I had stuck it out, though."

As their conversation stalled, Evan returned to their table with two pizza dough-wrapped burgers at hand. Tabby's appetite returned with a vengeance as she dug into the inventive burger inspired by the restaurant's namesake. Donnie tore into his dinner with matched enthusiasm and soon, they fell into a comfortable pattern of chewing and laughing together. When Evan slid the check across the table, Donnie snatched it up and insisted on paying.

"No, let me get my half!" she protested, reaching for her purse.

"Too late," he said, slipping three crisp twenties into the bill folder.

Tabby rummaged in her bag for her car keys, her face burning with embarrassment. She wasn't sure what to make of the current situation. The dinner that had started out feeling like a date was now *definitely* heading in that direction.

"Thanks," she said. "This was fun. I haven't gotten to hang out with a friend in a long time."

"Yeah, it's cool," Donnie said, rubbing the back of his head. "I know I'm your boss or whatever, but I think we can be friends too. Right?"

"Right," she said, breathing a sigh of relief. She rose to her feet and stuck out a blood-splattered hand. "Friends then?"

Donnie gazed down at her hand with a sad sort of smile and laughed. "Yeah," he said, accepting her reach. "Friends."

That same sweet and fluffy candy-filled sensation warmed through her body as his hand slid into hers. His palm was rough but warm against her skin, comfortable and familiar, but thrilling all at once. Before their handshake, Tabby was well aware that she wanted more from Donnie than friendship, but as their hands shook robotically up and down, there was no going back. She fluttered her false eyelashes up at him, wanting more than anything to reach up on her tiptoes and feel the scruff of his cheek against her palm. Instead, he only released her hand.

Disappointed, Tabby followed Donnie as they exited the restaurant, their dinner ending on a flat, unceremonious note. She spied Evan from the corner of her eye as he waved and mouthed the words "text me" from afar. Tabby wished that there was something to text him about.

"So I guess I'll see you tomorrow for opening night?" Donnie said, pulling a set of car keys from his pocket. Tabby stared into the faded, monster-emblazoned image on the front of his shirt. She wanted to bury her head in the soft contours of his chest and hug him. She wanted to continue fangirling with him about old horror movies and childhood haunts all night. She had found a friend in town to share her quirky passions with, but if she didn't play her cards right, she could ruin this good thing before it even began.

"I'll be there with birds on," she smiled.

Donnie nodded and smiled back. "Night, Tabby."

"Goodnight."

A full moon illuminated the late September sky as Tabby's vintage-style flats clacked along the sidewalk in time with her beating heart. She had plenty of other things that should be occupying her mind at that particular moment: the repairs that needed to be done to her mother's house, how she was going to pay for college, buying a car, getting her own place. She had a lot of hurdles to clear, all on top of quieting the voice in her head that told her to run away from it all again. Still, at that moment, the one thing that she really cared about was seeing Donnie again the following day. As she drove home that night, Tabby looked forward to working at the Haunted Hike more than almost anything else. The moon followed her all the way home as she pushed down her worries and dreamed instead of the nearby future filled with all things Halloween.

Chapter Eight

The opening week of Ty Treadwell's Haunted Hike attracted even more customers than Donnie could have dreamed of. The buy-one-get-one-free coupon ad he bought in the local paper likely had something to do with it, but still, the guests that came by the Fun Park that week exceeded their usual numbers. Sales at the go-karts, mini golf and batting cages were all up, as were sales at the concession stand. Normally, after payroll, they were lucky if the Haunted Hike broke even, but this year, Donnie's hard work was actually turning a profit.

The reviews from the local entertainment section of the News Press were more positive than usual as well, another side-effect that Donnie didn't expect. Tabby's costume even got a nod in the write-up, though the journalist did note that they needed to work on their parking situation. It was a valid argument; Donnie was still trying to figure out all of the logistics when it came to running the event a little more smoothly. However, with the profits from the Haunted Hike opening week, he was able to hire a few parking attendants to direct the overflow of traffic.

The long nights and extra mental toll from the Haunted Hike always left Donnie exhausted and exhilarated all at once. Even though he still doubted his ability to pull everything off, hearing the compliments and screams of delight from guests as he lurked in the manmade swamp brought a smile to his masked face. Donnie knew that designing sets and creating creepy atmospheres was what he was meant to do. It made him happier than anything in the world. Anything, that is, except for Tabby Peterson.

Working alongside Tabby every night at the Haunted Hike was akin to being back in school again. The anticipation he experienced before every shift left him feeling more nervous and giddy than usual, and not just because he was getting to scare not-so-unsuspecting hikers. Being near Tabby made his heart beat faster than a Rob Zombie bassline, and with every day that passed, it was getting harder and harder for him to hide his more than friendly feelings toward her.

It was well into the month of October when Tabby came into Ty Treadwell's Family Fun Park on a nondescript, do-nothing Tuesday morning. The light was beginning to change outside and the air was uncharacteristically crisp for southwest Florida. It was a rare, magical kind of day when one could almost imagine wearing a chunky sweater and stomping through leaves. Donnie was light and hopeful for once as he crunched numbers on the company laptop. He was making sense of the program that Melissa had been training him on, but lost all his focus as a familiar curvy silhouette came into view.

Immediately, Donnie's body went into fight or flight mode as he made himself look too busy to notice her. Even out of the corner of his eye, Tabby was impossible not to notice. From her hot pink hair to her floaty pumpkin-orange dress, she was a bright beacon in the darkened arcade. Even if she didn't look like the very picture of some kind of sexy Halloween fantasy, Donnie wouldn't have been able to ignore her energy. He was drawn to it like a moth to a flame.

"Hey Donnie," Tabby said, approaching the prize counter. He gazed up from his laptop and feigned surprise as she leaned over the glass and inspected the prize case. Donnie always made sure to carry the usual prizes that one would find at any family fun park behind the main reception area, including rubber bracelets, bouncy balls, invisible ink, stuffed animals, and keychains. However, since it was nearly Halloween, he also loaded up the prize case with pumpkin erasers, plastic vampire teeth, witch fingers, and other spooky little things for kids to collect in exchange for their hard-earned tickets. To Donnie's delight, his seasonally curated prizes caught her eye.

"Ooh, an eyeball ring!" she said, leaning over the case like one of his excited young patrons. Donnie leaned in as she pointed to the prizes. "Is that skull a stress ball? I think I could use one of those."

"You'll have to earn it," he said, throwing her a wicked grin. "Costs fifty tickets."

"No sweat," Tabby said, slapping a twenty dollar bill on the counter. "I'll take a hundred tokens."

Donnie slid her cash back across the counter. "Employees play for free," he said. "Your money's no good here."

"Nuh uh," she protested. "I'm going to win my prizes fair and square."

Donnie raised his eyebrows and didn't push the matter further. "If you insist," he said. "So what brings you in on your day off?"

Tabby shrugged. "I needed to get out of the house. Oh, and I wanted to celebrate. I passed my entrance exams."

"Nice!" Donnie said, handing over a baggie of tokens. "Congratulations."

"Thanks," Tabby said. "I won't start classes until next year, but that's okay. I need some time to figure out how I'm going to pay for it all anyway."

"Sounds like a good plan," Donnie said, leaning on the counter. "So, which games are you going to play?"

"Skee-Ball, obviously. Probably the jackpot wheel. I would play air hockey, but it doesn't look like there's anyone here to play me," she said, examining her tokens.

Donnie glanced around the empty arcade and then down at his spreadsheet. Payroll and taxes could wait.

"I could play you, if you want." He shrugged. "I mean, I'm not busy at the moment or anything."

"Really?" Tabby said, her face lighting up. "I don't want to take you away from your work."

"Nah. I'm ready for a break," he said, grabbing a bag of tokens for himself. "Besides, I need someone to help me test out the new first person shooter *Terminator* game."

"*The Terminator*?" she said, her face dead serious. Donnie couldn't be sure, but he could swear that her pupils dilated a little as a smile curled into the corner of her lips.

"Oh, it's *on.*"

Donnie hopped out from behind the counter with his bag of tokens in hand, feeling only slightly ridiculous. It had been quite some time since he enjoyed his own arcade games, and save from collecting tokens and refreshing the ticket rolls, Donnie never really had cause to touch them. Now, with Tabby gleefully at his side and a bag of coins at the ready, the urge to play was infectious.

"I always wanted to have a birthday party here as a kid," Tabby said, approaching the Skee-Ball machines. "I went to a few, but I never got to have one of my own here."

"Why not?"

"Well for one, it was too expensive. Plus, my birthday is on Halloween. No one wanted to give up trick-or-treating for a birthday party."

"What?" Donnie said, his eyes open wide. "You have a Halloween birthday? That's unbelievably cool."

Tabby shrugged. "I guess," she said. "I'm not that big on celebrating my birthday these days. But I still love Halloween."

"I had *all* of my birthdays here," Donnie scoffed, sliding a token into the machine. "It wasn't that great."

"So, why are you still here?" Tabby asked, picking up a Skee-Ball. "No offense, but it doesn't seem like you like your job that much."

Donnie frowned. "I dunno. It feels like my responsibility, I guess," Donnie said, rolling the Skee-Ball up the ramp. "Uncle Ty didn't have any kids, and he wanted to pass something down to me and Melissa. I didn't know what I wanted to do with my life, so I just kind of went with it."

"And at least you have the Haunted Hike." Tabby shrugged. "You've really made it better than I remember."

"Thanks," Donnie said, offering a half-smile. He rolled another Skee-Ball. "So, why did *you* come back to town?"

Tabby rolled her Skee-Ball into a hundred-point pocket and pumped her fist into the air.

"Security," she sighed. "It was time for a change. I want a cat. Some house plants. Health insurance. It's hard to have those things living like a nomad."

"Did you ever think of getting one of those tiny houses?" Donnie said. "You could be one of those van life hipsters."

Tabby shrugged. "Well, there's my mom I need to think about, too. She needs some help. I feel a little guilty for not being around for so long."

"Yeah. I understand the whole guilt thing," Donnie said, rolling his last Skee-Ball.

An hour passed in the blink of an eye as they shot basketballs, fielded air hockey pucks and smashed buttons. Every electronic victory was met with an enthusiastic high-five, and more than once, elbows and hips collided in a frenzied game play. When the last token had been spent, Tabby's fists were overflowing with red prize tickets ready for redemption.

"So, how many tickets do you think you racked up?" Donnie asked, following her back to the counter.

"At least three hundred," she guessed.

"Well, let's see what the ticket muncher has to say."

Donnie led her to his new ticket counting kiosk on the other side of the prize booth. It was expensive, but it had been a major time saver for him behind the counter. Tabby fed her tickets into the machine and it zipped them from her hand as the number on the electric reader climbed higher and higher.

"Can you believe some of these places don't give out prize tickets anymore?" she asked. "It's probably better for the environment to use rechargeable cards instead. Seems to take away the fun though."

"I know what you mean," he said. "Kids used to hoard their tickets for months to save up for the big prizes."

"That was me," Tabby laughed. "That's how I got my one and only lava lamp."

Donnie added his small amount of tickets to her final tally at the end. Tabby shook her head but didn't protest. When the ticket muncher finished doing its job it spat out a receipt with a tally of her winnings.

"Four hundred and eight," Donnie nodded. "Nice."

Tabby leaned over the prize counter with her winning receipt at hand. It was nearly noon and a few patrons had begun to wander in. Still, Donnie was happy to have spent his morning enjoying the arcade and her company.

"I'll take the rainbow slinky," she said, pointing in the case. "The squishy stress skull, of course. Ooh, that candy necklace aaaand... two pairs of vampire fangs, please."

Donnie collected her prizes and placed them on the counter in exchange for her receipt as his head and his heart struggled to agree. Their impromptu play session ended almost as soon as it began, and he was more confused than ever about what was going on between them. The chemistry between them was hot and tangible, and it took every ounce of his self-composure not to trip up. It was a bad position for him to be in, and with every shared laugh and accidental touch, his grip on the situation was getting looser.

"Hey," she said, slipping her winnings into her purse. "That was a lot of fun."

"Yeah, thanks for whipping my butt on *The Terminator*. I should call you Sarah Connor from now on."

"Ha ha," she said, smirking up at him from under a swish of candy colored hair. "I wish I knew you were this cool to hang out with back in high school."

He blinked and let out a nervous laugh. "Yeah, I wish we hung out back then too."

She smiled and bit her lower lip as she rocked back and forth on her heels. "Did you see that the drive-in off of old US-41 was playing the *Night of the Living Dead* series all month?"

Donnie cocked his head to the side as the blood in his veins turned to ice. Yes, *of course* he knew about it. He had been meaning to go, but getting away from the Family Fun Park in the evening was close to impossible. Between the look in her eyes and the way her perfectly glossed pink lips had formed the question, Donnie could guess what was coming next.

"Yeah, that looks pretty cool," he said, straightening his shoulders.

"They're showing *Night of the Living Dead* next Monday," she ventured. "I was wondering if maybe you would want to go?"

Donnie's heart thundered in his ears as the cogs in his brain processed the sudden turn in the conversation. A *date*. She was *definitely* proposing a date. Instantly, the thought of being alone in a darkened car with her, snuggled up watching a classic horror movie they both loved sounded like the best and worst thing in the world. He wanted to say yes. Oh, how he wanted to. His head wouldn't let him, though.

"I, uh — I don't know," he said, scratching the bridge of his nose. "Can I give you a maybe?"

Tabby's animated expression froze as she nodded. "Yeah! I mean, if you're too busy, I get it," she laughed.

"I want to," he said, the feeling leaving his legs. "I really do. I just have to check on some things first."

"It's fine! I — you know, don't worry about it. I feel silly for asking," she said, digging out her keys from her bag. "Anyway, thanks for playing today. I'll see you Thursday?"

"Yeah," he said. "See you Thursday."

Donnie's stomach plummeted to the floor as she waved and exited the arcade the way she came in. He blew it. Dumb Donnie Treadwell, friendzoned again, and this time by his own indecisive ass. Tabby turned and waved one last time as she exited into the beautiful autumn afternoon, a technicolor vision in Converse. Donnie stared down at his laptop again, right back where he started, only now with the fragrance of her cotton candy perfume in the air. He blew it when it came to Tabby Peterson, and if history repeated itself like it always did, this was one friendship faux pas from which he might not be able to bounce back.

Chapter Nine

"He said *no*?"

Evan held a foamy latte in one hand and a dish towel in the other as he stared incredulously at Tabby. It was the following Thursday morning and she had been mulling over her day trip to Ty Treadwell's Family Fun Park for the last two days. She felt silly for even going there on her day off in the first place, but Donnie had seemed happy to see her. They had fun for a while, and then she had to go and ruin everything by asking him to go to the drive-in. She was acting too eager. Too clingy. She was pushing him away.

"He said *maybe*," she moaned. "It was ridiculous of me to ask him anyway. He's my boss. I'm probably making him feel awkward."

"I saw you two at dinner the other night," Evan protested, setting down the coffee on the counter. "He looked *very* comfortable. Cinnamon spice latte for Ashley!"

"I know, I know," Tabby said, biting her lower lip. "He wouldn't hang out with me if he didn't want to."

"You two had *chemistry*. Like, hot, hot, chemistry," Evan said, mimicking a chef's kiss into the air. "Oh, I could have cut the tension between you two with a *knife*."

"So what am I doing wrong then?" Tabby said. "Not to sound conceited, but my approach usually works on guys. Maybe he's not romantically interested in me."

"Or, maybe he's being a gentleman," Evan said. "Workplace relationships can be a gray area. It's a strange landscape to navigate."

"I know. That's why I feel so bad. I should have left him alone," she said, leaning on the counter. "It's just... it's been a long time since I connected with someone like that. It's intoxicating, you know?"

Evan let out a deep sigh through his nose and frowned. "No, not really," he said. "But I'm keeping the hope alive."

Tabby gave him a sad half smile. "I suppose," she said. "At least I haven't scared you off yet."

"You're stuck with me until they hire me at The Royal Palm Dinner Theater," Evan said, adding a dollop of cream to the coffee he was preparing. "Caramel creme for Donna!"

"Oh, I'm off early again today," Tabby said, checking the time on her phone. "My uncle is coming by the house and I need to talk to him before my shift at the Haunted Hike tonight."

"Okay, but you owe me," Evan said. "There's an audition for *White Christmas* next week and I've been practicing my Bing Crosby impersonation."

"Deal," she said. "Tell me when and I'll cover for you."

"Go," Evan said, shooing her off. "And don't feel too bad about thirsting after your boss. You certainly wouldn't be the first."

"Thanks," Tabby laughed, untying her apron. "Okay, I'll see you bright and early tomorrow morning."

"Bye," Evan said, sliding another coffee on the counter. "Black coffee for Dennis!"

Tabby stepped out onto First Avenue where her mother's car was thankfully waiting at the curb. With Uncle Steve coming to the house in the afternoon, her mother had agreed to let her borrow the car so she could save time with her commute. Tabby had been counting the dollars and the days until she would be able to afford her own vehicle, and the gig at Ty Treadwell's had helped her savings grow. She approached her mother's tiny home to find her uncle standing in the driveway, his hands on his hips and eyes locked on the roof, her hopes faded.

"Hey Uncle Steve," Tabby said, slamming the car door behind her.

"Tabby," he said, embracing her in a hug. "Your hair's a different color every time I see you."

"I'm in disguise," she teased. "So? What's the damage?"

Her uncle removed the baseball cap from the top of his head and readjusted it before letting out a long, low breath. "It's not good. Probably looking at a thousand bucks to fix it."

"A thousand?" Tabby said, biting at her thumb's nail. "For the whole thing?"

"Yup," he said. "I can do the labor for you, but the materials alone are going to be expensive."

Tabby shook her head. "Mom can't do it," she said. "Her social security checks barely cover the electricity bill and groceries as it is."

"Well, this was my house growing up too," her Uncle Steve said, looking back up at the roof. "Your grandpa would have wanted me to help out. I can go half on it."

Tabby pursed her lips into a thoughtful, screwed up sort of expression. She didn't have a dime to spare if she was going to get a new car and her own apartment before the end of the year. On the other hand, she couldn't very well let her mother's house fall down on top of her either.

"Okay," she said. "Let's do it. But let me tell mom I'm paying for half. She won't let you do it if she thinks I'm spending any of my own money."

"Sounds like a plan," her uncle said. "I'm sorry I let things get this bad over here. I'm usually pretty busy over at my own place, but I feel responsible."

Tabby shrugged. "I didn't know it was this bad either. Thank you for coming out."

"No problem, kiddo," he said, leaning in for a hug again. "Your Aunt Stacy says hi. She wants to take you out to dinner for your birthday."

Birthday. Ugh. Tabby had been trying to forget.

"Sounds nice," she said. "Thanks."

Tabby untwisted the knots in her stomach as her uncle's engine roared to life. The screen door behind her slammed as Lucinda emerged onto the front porch, her mouth set into a thin line. They both waved as he pulled out onto the gravel drive leading up to the little home tucked away in the pine scrub forest. Tabby could already feel the strain of being set back financially once again, but it was something she couldn't help. She had spent a long time running away from responsibilities, and now she was going to pay for her conscience in drywall and roof shingles. She regarded her sweet mom who had always loved her and supported her no matter what and didn't feel a shred of regret.

"Uncle Steve is going to fix the roof," she said. "It's actually not as bad as it seems."

"That's good news." Her mom nodded.

"I need to go get ready for work," Tabby said, giving her a reassuring smile. "Thanks for letting me borrow your car again."

"Not like I'm using it anyway," her mom said. "I hope you're being careful out there in those woods."

"I am," she reassured her mother, looking up into the October sky. "It's not the woods I'm afraid of."

***

Time had a way of passing quickly for Tabby when she was having fun, and working the Haunted Hike was no exception. Days bled into weeks as she toiled away on double shifts, first at the cafe from 6 a.m. until 3 p.m., then at the Haunted Hike from 8 p.m. until after midnight. She picked up extra hours at the café covering for Evan during auditions and spent her little extra time helping Uncle Steve clean out her room in preparation for construction. And even though her energy and time were consumed with all of the plates that she was constantly balancing, her heart still hurt more than a little when it came to Donnie Treadwell.

Tabby didn't know what she expected to happen between her and the aloof Family Fun Park manager. She knew what she *wanted* to happen: she wanted to jump into his arms and spend lazy days off tangled under the covers and watching their favorite scary movies. She wanted to carve pumpkins with him and meander through the Haunted Hike hand-in-hand, pretending to be scared. Yes, she was a little lonely, but after some time had passed, she realized that she wasn't simply pining after Donnie because he was the closest, easiest option. He was sweet and kind and even if he didn't always know the right thing to do, she spied him from afar enough to tell that he was trying. In a way, they were both on the same level and trying to find out where they fit in a world that they didn't conform to. With Donnie, she felt seen, but it wasn't enough. She wanted to feel something else too.

It was on the Sunday before Halloween when they spoke again. More than a week had gone by and she and Donnie had only exchanged awkward pleasantries in passing. There wasn't much time to do anything else, though; the Haunted Hike had grown wildly popular and grew busier each night as Halloween neared. Still, her heart swelled with anticipation as the swamp creature ambled down the path toward her on that silent Sunday night.

"Hi," Donnie said, removing his gill-man mask. His hair was dripping with chlorinated water as Tabby smiled and propped her hands on her hips.

"Did you take a swim?" she asked.

"Yeah," he said. "A little kid pretended to take me out with a bow and arrow, so I had to play dead."

"Good call," she laughed. "What's up?"

Donnie sucked in a deep breath as he tucked the terrifying mask under his arm.

"I was wondering if you still wanted to go to the drive-in," he said, looking down at her under heavy, knit-together brows. "I understand if it's a no, but I've been thinking a lot and—"

"Yes," Tabby said, blurting out her answer without hesitation.

Donnie chuckled. "You didn't let me finish," he said, breaking into a smile. "I wanted to say yes the first time you asked, but I didn't know if it would be... appropriate."

"Because you're my boss?" she asked.

Donnie nodded.

"Well, I'm only going to work for you for like another week," she shrugged. "Plus, we're consenting adults here, right?"

"I didn't want you to think there was any other reason I didn't say yes right away," he said. "I'm not into playing games like that."

"I don't know," Tabby shrugged. "You were pretty good at Skee-Ball."

"Har har," Donnie said, rolling his eyes. "So, tomorrow night?"

Tabby's entire body thrummed as she eyed Donnie through the dark. The shrieks of the last Haunted Hike walkers filled the air as the slash pine branches overhead swayed in the cool October breeze. Tiny little sparkles danced up her spine as a long-forgotten sensation warmed her insides. It was the same sensation she had experienced so many nights ago trick-or-treating with friends. The days leading up to Christmas. The morning of a much-awaited trip to a theme park. Excitement. Anticipation.

"Yeah, tomorrow night works for me," Tabby said, attempting to look cool and collected.

"I can pick you up at your place?" he offered. "Around seven?"

"I'll meet you here," she said, perhaps a little too quickly. "It'll be easier that way."

"Oh, sure," Donnie said, pulling a plastic sandwich baggie out of his pocket. It was dripping wet from his costume, but the small white card on the inside remained intact. Tabby accepted the baggie from him with a curious frown.

"That's my new business card," he said, beaming down at her. "The, uh, the one that says cell is obviously my cell phone. You can just text me if something comes up and you can't make it."

"Oh, I'll be there," Tabby said, smiling down at the card through the damp baggie. "Donald Treadwell. Manager, Owner and CEO. Very official."

"I know. It sounds ridiculous," he said. "Anyway. I have to go close up the hike for tonight."

"Okay," Tabby said, her insides still firing off like sparklers. "Good night."

"Night."

Tabby stood and sighed as Donnie jogged down the path, leaving her with the wet baggy in one hand and her heart in the other. A soft, light touch caressed her cheek and a small yelp escaped from her throat. Two dark, beady eyes stared back at her as she breathed a sigh of relief. The black bird pinned to her shoulder scared her at least once every time she dressed in her Alfred Hitchcock-inspired ensemble.

"See, I told you Edgar," she said, to the inanimate raven. "Looks like tomorrow, I've got a date."

Chapter Ten

Donnie had almost forgotten how to get ready for a date. It had been a long time since he had been on one, maybe a little too long. Even though his game was rusty, Tabby inspired him to put in some good effort. He knew to take care of the basics: shower, comb hair, clean nails, wear a nice shirt and pants. Brush teeth, rinse with mouthwash and pack some gum in case of emergencies or breath-offending snacks. Only when he opened his truck door that evening, Donnie realized that he had forgotten one majorly important detail.

Oh my god, he thought to himself, eyeing the interior of his truck. *I can't pick her up in this.*

The interior of his old, outdated truck was littered with the usual suspects: empty coffee cups, junk mail, and more than a few months worth of dirt. There was no time to hit a car wash and properly scrub his truck and vacuum the floor boards, so a quick shake of the rugs, a swipe at his dusty console and a garbage haul was the best he could do. He started up the engine and said a silent prayer that it would be too dark for Tabby to notice his pigsty of a vehicle.

The sun was beginning to do its nightly dance behind the twisted treeline at Ty Treadwell's when he arrived that evening. His sweaty palms flexed against the wheel as he recognized Tabby's car already parked in the lot. Donnie must have parked in that very same lot a million times, but now, as he turned into the spot across from Tabby's car, it was like he had never operated a vehicle before. Still, he managed to slide into a spot and shift into park without doing too much ruin to his truck or his nerves.

"Hi," Tabby said, smiling up at him, all teeth and sparkling eyes. Her hair glowed even brighter than usual, the length grazing her exposed collarbone in a way that made him feel inappropriate for looking. She was dressed in a pair of black skinny jeans and some kind of off-the-shoulder top that showcased a crop of tattoos that he didn't know she had. He struggled to keep an even keel as his eyes tried not to wander.

"You look nice," Donnie said, somehow managing to keep his line of sight up. "Did you get something done to your hair?"

"Yeah," she laughed, smoothing down the top of her head. "These special hair colors fade pretty fast. Plus, I needed a trim. You look nice, too."

"Well, I was going to get this thing dyed and trimmed too," Donnie said, stroking his beard. "I don't think pink would look so good on me."

"Won't know until you try," she laughed, approaching the truck with a wink.

He rounded the other side of his truck on wobbly knees and opened the door for Tabby to enter. As she floated past him, Donnie detected a subtle whiff of her candy-scented perfume or body lotion and knew for certain that he was in trouble. He normally didn't care for heavy fragrances, but Tabby's was light, sweet and nostalgic. Being around her whisked him back to a simpler time. *Everything* about Tabby had that effect on him.

When Donnie got behind the wheel, it became apparent that there was one particularly embarrassing relic that he had forgotten to clear from his truck. Tabby was settled into her seat, her eyes glued to his giant book of CD's. It was the same book that had been jammed under his passenger side seat for the last fifteen years and contained an embarrassing catalog of music that he hadn't listened to in years. His blood instantly went cold as she flipped through the pages and laughed at the weathered old discs in the giant binder.

"Donnie! Oh my gosh!" she said, clutching her chest. "Is this a Surge Soda CD?"

Donnie's face flamed. He cringed and peered over her shoulder. "Yeah," he admitted. "I had to drink a dozen cases of that stuff to get it."

"Look at all of these soundtracks," Tabby said, gleefully scanning the dozens of disks. "Does your CD player still work?"

"I think so," he said, turning on his engine. "I haven't listened to any of those in a long time."

"Cake, Mr. Bungle, Primus... there's some interesting options in here," she said, pulling out a disc. "Ooh, a burned disc."

Donnie's head whipped around as he exited the parking lot.

"Actually, that's a good one," he said. "My Ultimate Halloween Playlist."

"Let's check it out," she said, pushing the disc into the player.

"Don't say I didn't warn you," Donnie said, trying to remember all the songs he had downloaded.

As they headed toward the drive-in movie theater, the ominous sound of church organs filled the truck, followed by a cackle and a blood-curdling screech. Tabby clapped as the intro made its way to a succession of classic horror movie songs and themes that Donnie had mashed together from his home computer so many Halloweens ago. As they sped down US-41, the combination of creepy music, Tabby's heavenly aroma, and the low, orange glow of an October sunset imprinted permanently in his mind. For the first time that night, as Tabby swayed along to the electronic music and the asphalt flew by beneath his tires, Donnie relaxed and enjoyed the moment. It was the happiest he had been in a long, long time.

Chapter Eleven

"I doused the popcorn in butter. Is that okay?"

Donnie returned to the truck right in time to hear Tabby's favorite line of classic zombie dialogue sound over the speaker. The old drive-in theater dated back to the 1960s when the idea of watching a movie from inside your car was more normal than kitsch. It was a place that Tabby had enjoyed visiting with her mom as a kid to watch second runs of movies for a dollar, and was one of the last of its kind for miles. Tabby gladly accepted the hot bag of popcorn as *Night of the Living Dead* played on the screen before them, and it occurred to Tabby that this probably wasn't the first time that this movie had flashed on that screen.

"They're coming to get you, Barbara," Johnny said onscreen.

"I love extra butter," Tabby said, popping a kernel into her mouth. Donnie handed her a soda as he slid back behind the seat of his truck, eyes glued to the screen. The waxy red and white cup was already drenched with condensation and she gladly slurped down a sweet, carbonated sip.

"I never get sick of watching this part," he said. "It's so simple, but so effective, you know?"

"Definitely," Tabby said, reaching into the bag. "Still holds up."

A soft, gentle hum vibrated through Tabby's entire being, the dialogue from the movie crackling over Donnie's stereo. Even though their drive-in movie date was loaded with expectation, she didn't feel all that nervous. Being with Donnie was easy and fun, like picking up with an old friend that she never knew she had. It was only when his fingers would accidentally brush against hers in the bag of popcorn, or their eyes would lock into place, that the fluttery, heart-stopping, punch-in-the-guts feelings began.

"Better run, Barbara," Donnie said, shaking his head. "Man, her brother is a *jerk*."

65

"Yeah! I always thought so too," she said, taking a sip of her soda. Tabby nodded in agreement as the brother and sister duo onscreen bickered while a sinister figure lurked in the distance. They sat in silence for a moment. As the familiar black and white zombie movie continued to play out on the screen, Tabby anticipated every beat. With every brush of their fingers in the shared bag of popcorn, she grew more and more giddy, as though they were two teenagers on a date and not a couple approaching thirty-something. There was no denying that one of the things that made Donnie so attractive to her was that just being near him made her feel something again, something special. An unnamed feeling she assumed was lost came rushing back, consuming her all over again.

"So is this the same truck you've had since you were a teenager?" Tabby asked, taking a sip of soda.

"Hmm?" Donnie tore his gaze away from the screen. "Oh yeah. How did you know?"

"You still have a THS sticker on your bumper," she smiled. "Plus, I remember you tearing out of the school parking lot in this thing."

Donnie snorted. "Yeah, it was brand new back then. Early graduation gift from Uncle Ty," Donnie said. "It's still running, so I don't see any reason to get a new one."

"That's smart," Tabby said, hesitating. She glanced over at Donnie, still happily munching on popcorn. There was something she had been wanting to say from the minute they reconnected. Something that was true, but seemed maybe a little too much to confess all at once. Still, if she didn't say it, she feared the words would burst out of her at an inopportune time. It was something she owed it to herself to say to him. Something he needed to hear.

"I wish I knew you back when we were in high school," Tabby ventured.

"Huh?" Donnie said. "You *did* know me."

"No, I mean like... I wish I *knew* you. I wish that I knew that we had the same CDs, and liked the same movies. Things might have been different."

"Why didn't you then?" he asked.

Tabby shrugged. "I don't know. I didn't see you like that. I had a different idea of who I thought you were."

"Oh? How'd you see me?" Donnie asked, a slight smirk on his face. "Just some dumb, rich kid with a famous uncle?"

"No!" Tabby protested, her eyes growing wide. "Well. I mean, you were pretty popular."

"It's okay," Donnie shrugged. "That's how a lot of other kids thought of me."

"Everybody loved you," Tabby said, shaking her head. "Didn't you get voted as the class clown in the yearbook? What about Dustin Sanchez? Mike Burkette? Eddie Fulton? You guys were always messing around together."

Donnie let out a low, bitter chuckle. "Yeah, and where are they now? I don't hear from any of them."

Tabby pursed her lips together and frowned. The air in the cab grew thick and uncomfortable. For a heart-stopping moment, she worried that she had ruined the conversation.

"I'm sorry if I brought up a sore subject," she said, completely forgetting about the movie now. "I think it's nice that you still have your truck from high school. I never even got a car."

"It's okay," he said, looking at her under heavy brows. "You know what's funny? Back then, I would have never thought you'd have given me the time of day."

Tabby's brows knitted together in confusion as she struggled to figure him out. He was smiling at her again, his face aglow in the light of the drive-in screen. "Me?"

"Yeah, you," Donnie said, leaning a little closer. "You had a nose ring. Dated older guys. All the girls feared you."

"They did *not*," Tabby said, feigning surprise. "I mean, I guess I could be a little intimidating back then."

Donnie got quiet and stared at the screen again as Tabby frowned at her soda. She couldn't tell if their date was going well or if it was turning into an absolute trainwreck. Even though they were at a drive-in watching a scary movie — the very stereotype of what a romantic date was *supposed* to be — the mood inside the truck was confusing. Part of the problem was that Donnie's attention was miles away. The other problem was the giant bag of popcorn in between them. Something had to give.

Tabby grabbed the bag of half-finished popcorn and placed it on the floor of the cab as the zombies onscreen descended upon the farmhouse. As the movie characters screamed and scrambled, she scooted to the center of the truck and made herself comfortable. Donnie gave her a side-eye of surprise, his shoulders squared up and tense.

"I have to tell you something," she said. "I had a massive crush on you back then. An embarrassingly, hugely, massive crush. It's how I came to love the Haunted Hike. I thought you might be there, and so I always went every year... looking for you."

Donnie huffed and sighed all at once, as though in disbelief or relief. She turned her hand over in her lap with her palm up in invitation and gazed into his utterly confused, handsome face. His shoulders and expression softened, as warm, rough fingers slid over her hand and locked into place. Their shoulders brushed and he gave her hand a gentle squeeze while zombies tormented and chased unsuspecting victims in the distance.

"It was me, you know. With the chainsaw and the mask," Donnie said. "I looked for you every year at the Haunted Hike too."

Tabby blinked as she recalled the terrifying finale to the Haunted Hike. The looming figure in a hockey mask with a chainless chainsaw buzzing in the air. She was always the one that was chased, even as her girlfriends went screaming through the pathway in front of her. It had been him all along. Of *course* it was him.

"*You* were the chainsaw jerk at the end of the walk!" Tabby said, her mouth open in surprise. "Why didn't you ever tell me —"

All of Tabby's sensibilities temporarily suspended as Donnie leaned in, smelling of laundry hung out to dry and something spicy and masculine. This was really happening, this moment that she had been obsessing over since she signed up for the Haunted Hike. Since high school, really. With the heady aroma of salty, buttery popcorn still lingering in the air, she gazed up at Donnie and searched his eyes. He held back, his face hovering mere inches from her, waiting as her body burned with anticipation. She nodded and tilted her chin up at him in expectation, shoulders pressed tightly together and their hands firmly clasped. Tabby reached up with her free hand and found the scruff of his cheek surprisingly pleasant to touch, smooth and prickly all at once. When she couldn't stand it any longer, Tabby guided his lips to hers in a soft, sweet embrace that was a lifetime in the making.

Their kiss was slow and gentle at first, exploratory and only a little awkward. It had been ages since Tabby had taken part in a front seat makeout session. More than once, she banged a knee against the dashboard as she edged closer to him. Despite his initial hesitance, Donnie matched her intensity as arms and hands roamed over every inch of her body. Several times, Donnie's elbow nearly laid down on the horn as the forgotten movie on the screen cast shadows down on them. After a few moments of frenzied but uncomfortable and awkward making out, Tabby had enough.

"That's it," she gasped, coming up for air.

"What?" Donnie said, letting out a deep sigh. "Are you okay? Did I do something wrong?"

Tabby glanced in the back seat as a wicked grin spread across her lips. The windows were heavily tinted and nearly all fogged, perfect for what she had in mind. She eyed the interior of the cab and stared at

Donnie again as she crawled through the space in between the front and back seat. Donnie laughed and turned to face her as her hands shot through from the back seat and curled around the collar of his shirt.

"What are you doing?" he laughed as she guided him through the space. With a little effort, he was able to maneuver through and join her in the much roomier back seat.

Tabby's heart raced in her ears as she smiled back at him in the dark. It had been a long, long time since she had done anything like this. She tugged her shirt over her head as his eyes remained glued to her form, a permanent grin transfixed on his face. The way he looked at her, hungry and surprised all at once, only added to her excitement.

"Trick or treat, Donnie," she said, dropping her shirt to the floor.

His eyes widened as she lowered one black bra strap and then another. Tabby laughed as she crawled across the back seat toward him, propelled by a whole new sensation. Donnie smiled as she straddled him without a care in the world in their own private haven.

"Oh my god," he said, cupping her face with his hands. "Happy freakin' Halloween."

Chapter Twelve

For the rest of the week leading up to Halloween, Donnie strutted around the grounds of Ty Treadwell's Family Fun Park like a prize rooster. All of the little things that usually bothered him or caused him anxiety or stress were muted as he went about his day and took care of his responsibilities. The sky was brighter. Music sounded better. Food tasted amazing. It was his favorite time of year, and he was in the thick of it, doing his favorite things. And, for the first time in a very long time, Donnie Treadwell had a girlfriend.

It was strange to call Tabby his girlfriend, especially since it had been a long time since she had been a girl, or since he had been a boy, for that matter. Still, he couldn't deny that she made him feel young again. Being around Tabby was nothing short of intoxicating. For the first time in a long time, he had something to look forward to again with her in the world. Even though he had dated on and off, none of the women he had been set up with or met online had made him feel quite so connected. With Tabby, it was like an internal switch had been flicked on and set to full power, and with every passing day he grew more and more drunk off their shared electric vibes.

It didn't take long for gossip about the new couple to spread through the Haunted Hike staff. He and Tabby didn't exactly try to hide their affection for one another either, stealing kisses between shifts on the trail, at the lagoon or in the cemetery. Still, the whispers about them before and after each night of scaring didn't seem malicious or bearing ill-will at all. Before long, the final night of the Haunted Hike was nearing, as was his annual Halloween house party for all of his employees.

Donnie was still learning the ropes when it came to running a business, but when it came to throwing a party, he had no problem pulling out all the stops. The home that he shared with his Uncle Ty overlooking the Caloosahatchee River was admittedly the perfect location for a big Halloween bash. With an Olympic-sized on-grounds pool, surround sound speaker system, and an outdoor kitchen and fireplace, Uncle Ty's house made entertaining friends and family easy. Tabby proved to be an enthusiastic co-planner and decorator, as they happily spent all of Halloween Eve morning lining the back porch with orange and black streamers and hanging fake spider webs in every corner. By early afternoon, the house was party-ready and Donnie could sit back and relax a little. The Haunted Hike had wrapped up a successful season, and he was more than ready to celebrate. The DIY swamp creature mask he had lovingly created was beginning to fall apart, as was his body after spending night after night stalking around his lagoon. Even though he loved the Haunted Hike more than almost anything, he was ready to put it all away for the season and get down to the business of enjoying Halloween.

"Okay, so how many people RSVP'd for tonight?" Tabby asked, pen poised in the air.

"About thirty people from the Haunted Hike? Then of course there's Melissa and her wife, and a few other friends. I think maybe forty people will be here, tops?"

"Better order ten pizza's," Tabby nodded, jotting down the information on a pad of paper. "Now we just need to get out the ice, drinks, chips, candy... what else?"

"Oh yeah, apples for apple bobbing," Donnie said. "I almost forgot."

"Ew! Like, in a vat of water? Where everyone slobbers all over everything? That kind of apple bobbing?" Tabby said, making a face.

"No," Donnie laughed. "That's definitely not sanitary. We figured out a way to do it where you tie the apples on strings and people have to bite them mid-air. It's pretty hilarious."

"Love it," Tabby said, relieved.

"I also got stuff to make Melissa's favorite Franken-punch," he said. "It's basically ginger ale and vodka with green food coloring and dry ice."

"Sounds dangerous," Tabby laughed.

"Thank you for helping me today, by the way," Donnie said. "It's nice to have someone else to share this with. My folks are pretty religious, so they don't do Halloween."

"I didn't know that," Tabby said, putting down her pen.

"Yeah, I don't exactly get along with them. That's why I came to live with Uncle Ty in the first place," Donnie said. "I probably should be out on my own by now, but his place is pretty nice."

"I know the feeling," Tabby said. "I'm going through that now being back home too. Only my mom loves Halloween. She always made my costumes for me."

"Your mom sounds pretty great," Donnie said, wrapping his arms around her waist.

Tabby's eyes softened as she sunk into his embrace. "She is."

Donnie blinked as her shoulders trembled against him. Hot tears had sprung up in the corner of her eyes and sank into the fabric of his shirt. "What's wrong?" he asked, brushing a hot pink strand of hair from her eyes.

Tabby's face was red and screwed up into a pained frown as he squeezed her tighter. "I should have never left her, you know?" she sniffed, her voice strained. "Now things are so bad..."

"Hey, it's okay," he said, even though he didn't actually know if that was true. Donnie struggled to find the words as she sobbed into his chest. He immediately wanted to fix everything for her as panic flooded his chest. Listening was the best he could do for now.

"Her house is falling apart," Tabby said, her voice muffled in the crook of his arm. "She doesn't have a job or any friends. She just sits in her house all day making things with yarn. I feel awful."

Donnie bit his lip, wishing he knew the right thing to say. Her words hit him right in his own soft spot. The guilt he had for leaving his family as a teen was a deep, deep wound that he never talked about unless Melissa pried it out of him. But now was not the time to dump his baggage on her.

"Well, you're back here now," he said, cradling her face in his hands. He wiped a fat tear from her cheek with the pad of his thumb. "I'm sure she's happy about that."

Tabby nodded and wiped at her face. "I need to get some things settled so I can finally start my life," she said. "But I feel so trapped at home."

"Well, you'll have your own car soon," he reasoned. "You'll get your own place. Then you can still be close to her but set some healthy boundaries."

Tabby sucked in a deep breath. "Yeah, we'll see," she said, looking up at him with a forced smile. "Sorry. I don't know where all of that came from."

"It's okay," he said, planting a kiss on her forehead. "Don't ever feel like you have to hide that kind of stuff from me."

Tabby nodded up at him, her eyes still glassy with tears. "Okay, that's enough of that," she said, checking the time on her phone. "I need to go get ready. People are going to be here soon."

"I guess I should go get into costume too," Donnie said. "I hate that you won't tell me what you're going to dress up as."

"Good," she said, giving him a playful shove. "You won't have to stand the torture for much longer."

Donnie sighed to himself as Tabby disappeared into the house and turned his gaze to the skeleton seated by the door. He stared back at the plastic decoration, its eye sockets watching his every move. He nodded at the bony decor and returned its toothy grin.

"Gonna be an epic party tonight," he said, throwing the skeleton a thumbs-up. "I can feel it."

***

Donnie stared back at his reflection in the mirror and almost regretted his costume decision. It had been a long time since he had been clean-shaven, but he only nicked himself with the razor once. He wasn't completely bare-faced though, as the effect he was going for required a full mustache. He sighed and slid the baseball cap on top of his head, sucked in his gut and tucked the jersey into the pair of ridiculous white pants. Even though he was slightly uncomfortable in the getup, he had to admit, it was an effective transformation. He was the spitting image of his Uncle Ty's most famous MVP baseball card.

"Are you ready?" Tabby asked, her voice muffled on the other side of the door. He cringed at his reflection one last time.

"I guess," he said.

"Okay, open on three," she said. "One, two, three!"

Donnie took a deep breath and opened the door. His jaw nearly hit the floor as Tabby stood proudly on the other side with her hands on her hips. A giant black bouffant of a wig had been placed on top of her head, and her eyes were slathered in batwing liner and mascara. But it was the slinky black dress with a revealing, plunging neckline that really caught Donnie's attention.

"Elvira!" he said. "Yes!"

Tabby laughed as her hands flew to her blood red lips. "You look *exactly* like your uncle!" she said. "Hilarious!"

Donnie ran his thumb and forefinger along his freshly-shaven jawline. "You don't hate it?" he asked.

"*No*," she said, running her hands along the side of his face. "I *love* the mustache."

Donnie's heart pumped hot and fast in his veins as she planted a kiss on his lips. At that moment he was regretting inviting anyone over at all. As he was getting ready to round third base with Elvira, the doorbell rang.

"No," he groaned. "Not yet."

"Be a good sport," she teased.

It was nearly dark as the first wave of guests arrived, most dressed in costume. Some of the Haunted Hike employees came as their on-trail characters, and others opted for different costumes all together. Melissa and Stephanie dressed as twin bumblebees and burst into laughter as soon as Donnie came into view.

"Where is Uncle Ty?" Melissa asked, adjusting her antenna. "Has he seen you yet?"

"No. He's in Vegas with his new girlfriend," Donnie said. "He knew I was borrowing his jersey though."

"Where's the Franken-punch?" Melissa asked. "This is too uncanny. I need a drink."

Donnie shook his head. "Right this way."

As his Ultimate Halloween Playlist sounded over the pool speakers, Donnie searched through the sea of bodies to find Tabby at the stereo. She waved from across the room as a succession of zombies, vampires and other creatures of the night mingled on the patio. He pursed his lips and waved back, his bushy new mustache twitching as a lump formed in his throat. As his very own Elvira smiled back at him with the sounds of Halloween, fun and friends hanging thick in the air, Donnie's heart swelled. In that perfect, spooky sweet moment, he was happy and content. It was a moment he was determined to hold onto with both hands for a very long time.

Chapter Thirteen

Tabby swayed to the beat of the spooky love song that echoed through the air, her silky black dress swishing against her skin. She pressed her cheek to Donnie's chest and glanced up at him from under her hefty wig with a smile. Without his beard, he reminded her more than ever of the snarky kid she used to know, and part of her secretly hoped that he would keep the ironic mustache after Halloween was over. She laid her head against the scratchy material of his baseball jersey and sighed.

"I think this is the best Halloween party I've ever been to," she said. "Thanks, Donnie."

"Well, it ain't over yet," he said, leaning her over for a dramatic dip. Tabby braced her tall wig with one hand and laughed. He helped prop her upright as the world spun around and around.

"Have you had any of Melissa's famous Franken-punch yet?"

Tabby nodded as her vision continued to swim. "Yeah," she said. "It's pretty strong."

"Don't worry. I can drive you home if you need me to," he said, raising her hand in the air. He wound his arm around, twirling her in a circle as the ragged hemline of her dress flared out dramatically. Stars floated past her eyes.

"I better sit," she said, fanning herself.

"Good idea," Donnie said, leading her over to the patio furniture set. Tabby gratefully plopped down in the soft cushions and tried not to close her eyes as the party continued to spin.

"Do you need some water?" he asked.

Tabby nodded.

"I'll be right back," he said.

A green sort of gurgly sensation rose in her stomach as she rested on the couch and listened to the vibrant, cheerful din of the party. It had been a good night up to that point. Really good. She mingled with some of the new friends that she had made working the Haunted Hike.

She cheered Melissa and Donnie on as they both went head-to-head in the apple bobbing contest. She had also indulged in perhaps a little too much Franken-punch. Now it was all catching up to her, and Tabby feared that her night of fun was probably over.

"I didn't know if you wanted ice," Donnie said, returning with a glass of water. He placed the glass into her hand, his face wracked with worry. "I can get you some if you —"

Donnie was cut off as the lights on the back porch went out. The music stopped and a glowing orb floated toward them. Tabby didn't know if she was hallucinating or if something bad was about to happen.

"Happy birthday to you!" Melissa sang, her black and yellow bumblebee costume coming into view.

"Happy birthday to you," the rest of the party joined in. "Happy birthday dear Tabby, happy birthday to you!"

Tabby forced a smile as a giant, glowing sheet cake was placed in front of her. Covered in purple and black frosting, the cake featured a haunted house decoration with the words "Happy Birthday Tabby" written out in cursive icing. Donnie mouthed the words "I'm sorry" to her as she struggled to stay upright. She blew out the candles and everyone clapped before the worst waves of nausea set in. Another gurgle.

"Sorry, excuse me."

Tabby rose from the couch and pushed past confused party guests with a hand clamped over her mouth. She raced on wobbly knees toward the bathroom with her vision in a blur of orange, black and green. The last thing she heard before she slammed the bathroom door was Donnie calling out her name and the hushed sounds of concern.

***

"Everything okay in there?"

Tabby lifted her head from the toilet seat, her Elvira wig abandoned in a heap on the floor. Okay? No. At that moment, Tabby didn't think she would ever be okay again. She didn't know if it was possible as she could sense herself becoming even more drunk by the minute.

"No," she moaned.

"Can I come in?"

Tabby frowned as she evaluated her current situation. It had been a long time since she had drank like that, though she didn't think that she had much at the time. Melissa kept pouring cups full of the bubbling, potion-like punch and she kept going back for more. She was having such a good time and managed to screw it all up. She couldn't even enjoy her birthday cake.

"Yeah."

Tabby slumped against the wall, her feet cold against the tile floor. She lowered her eyes as Donnie slipped into the bathroom and closed the door behind him. She was ashamed to let him see her this way: drunk, sick and in a crumpled ball. She messed up, and Donnie had a front row seat.

"Can I get you anything?" he asked.

Tabby shook her head.

"Listen, I'm sorry about the cake," he said. "Melissa got over excited. If I knew she was bringing it out, I would have stopped her."

"It's okay," she said, trying to give him a smile. "It was sweet of you to get me a cake. I'm sorry I puked at your Halloween party."

"Nobody saw it," he reassured her. "Trust me, you wouldn't be the first to barf at one of these things. I should have warned you better about the Franken-punch."

"It's evil!" she laughed. "It tasted really good at the time. Now I just want to lay here and die."

"No," he said. "Do you want me to take you home? You can go lay down in one of the guest rooms too, if you want."

Tabby frowned at her options. Of *course* she wanted to stay at Donnie's fancy waterfront mansion. But she had already promised her mother that she would be home that night so they could have breakfast together in the morning. The idea of Donnie driving her home and actually seeing where she lived was out of the question too.

"I'll call a cab," she said, waving him off. "I don't want you to have to leave your party."

"It's not a problem," he said, extending a hand. "Let me help you up."

Tabby's head throbbed as she accepted his reach and wobbled to her feet. The familiar intro to *Thriller* blared over the pool speakers down the hall and she moaned at herself. If she wasn't already reeling and dizzy from overdoing it on Franken-punch, she would have been burning with embarrassment.

"I don't usually do this," she explained as he gathered her wig from the floor.

"Do what?" he asked, leading her through the house. Tabby took one last glance at the party as a heavy feeling settled into her heart.

"Get smashed," she said, gripping his arm. "I hate this feeling."

"It's fine, really," he said. "I just want to make sure you're okay."

"Everything all right?" Melissa, now missing the top half of her bumblebee costume, descended upon them with a look of concern.

"I'm going to take Tabby home. She's not feeling well. Can you wrap up the party if I'm not back in time?"

"Sure," Melissa said, her expression lined with worry. "Too much Franken-punch?"

"Yeah."

"Sorry," she said. "I won't make you drink any next year."

Next year, Tabby thought to herself as she gave Melissa a weak wave goodbye. *Will I even be here next year?*

As Donnie helped her up into his truck at the end of his long, massive driveway, the sounds of the party seemed distant and far away. She took one last look at his home and squeezed her eyes shut. Perfect landscaping. A huge front lawn. The tiered fountain that made way to a two-story Mediterranean-style mansion. As her head continued to swim, all Tabby could think of was what Donnie would say when he pulled up in front of her house.

She nodded in and out of consciousness as they drove through the night, the events of the evening playing out in fuzzy reruns. Donnie smiling down at her with his ridiculously adorable mustache. Mingling with new friends from the Haunted Hike. Dancing with Donnie. Everyone singing happy birthday. By all accounts, it was a great night up until that point, but in her drunken haze, it was hard for her to see anything but how badly she had screwed up. However, when Donnie reached the rugged, unpaved drive leading up to her home she had a whole new thing to dread.

"Whoa," he laughed as his truck bumped along in the dark. "It's kind of like a horror movie out here!"

Tabby sat up from her leaning position against the door, clutched the handle and gritted her teeth. Donnie wasn't wrong. Tabby had the same scary ideas herself a number of times as she had returned to her mother's house late at night. In the back of her mind, she was always ready for a Florida panther or a man in a mask to jump out at her from the palmetto bushes that surrounded their home way out in the pine scrub backwoods. After what seemed like an eternity of being jostled around in the cab of Donnie's truck, the front porch light came into view.

Instantly, Tabby regretted everything that she had done that night to lead her to this point as she viewed her childhood home in Donnie's headlights. Her mother's house was the exact opposite of where Donnie lived, with a giant blue tarp and sandbags that covered most of the roof where her uncle was working to repair the leak. The paint on the front porch was peeling. Their screen door was rusted and sagging at the hinges. Tabby was always a little bit embarrassed about where she lived, but her inebriated state only amplified her shame.

"Is this it?" Donnie asked, double-checking the map on his phone.

"Yep. This is where I live," she said, her voice monotone and flat.

"Here, I'll help you out —"

"Please don't," she said, digging through her purse. "Thank you for driving me home."

Tabby found her keys and sighed as she opened the door. She paused for a moment and glanced over at Donnie, his face illuminated in the overhead light of the cab. She should have leaned over to kiss him goodbye at least; she should have done something to reassure him and wipe the look of worry from his face. Instead, she froze up and turned into herself, too fuzzy-headed to find the right words.

"Good night," she said, only managing a weak smile.

"Good night," he said.

Tabby closed the door on Donnie's disappointed, confused expression and took careful steps up the gravel path to her front porch. Donnie continued to idle in the driveway until she opened the door before he backed out into a three-point turn and drove off the way that he came. She stood in the doorway as his headlights disappeared into the woods and her heart sank. A barred owl hooted somewhere in the distance as Tabby closed the door on what should have been a perfect night.

***

Tabby awoke the following morning to the smell of pumpkin pancakes and fresh coffee. She sat up on the couch and stretched, still dressed in her Elvira costume from the night before. It was Halloween morning, and Lucinda was busy in the adjacent kitchen making her traditional birthday breakfast. It was normally her favorite day in the entire year, but she didn't feel much like celebrating.

"Good morning, birthday girl," her mother said, bringing over a cup of coffee. "Rough night?"

Tabby managed a smile and accepted the mug. It warmed her hands, and the fragrant, spicy scent of the coffee creamer hit her nose in a pleasant way.

"Yeah. Donnie had to drive me home."

"I know," she said. "He called and said he would be bringing my car by this afternoon."

"He called the house?" Tabby said, nearly snorting coffee up her nose. "You spoke to him?"

"Yes, he seems very nice. He was worried about you."

"I know," Tabby moaned.

Her mother returned to the couch with a plate piled high with orange pancakes topped with butter and dripping in syrup. "What're your plans for today, birthday girl?"

Tabby shrugged. "I don't know. Now that the Haunted Hike is over, I should probably start looking for another job."

Her mother frowned. "You should go do something fun," she said. "You don't have any plans at all?"

Tabby shook her head. "Nope."

Lucinda pursed her lips and sat back in her seat as Tabby forced down her breakfast. She still wasn't feeling the best from her green punch drinking binge the night before, but she didn't want to disappoint her mother.

"Tabby," she said. "I asked your uncle where the money was coming from to fix the roof."

Her mother cleared her throat as Tabby put down her fork. She chewed and took a sip of coffee.

"Yeah?"

"Tabitha, you can't spend your own money on me!"

"I can afford it, mom," she said. "The roof needs to be fixed."

"I know, but I'm not helpless," her mother said, standing to her feet. "Besides, you need your own car more than I need you and your uncle to conspire behind my back."

Pinpricks of adrenaline flooded Tabby's legs as her eyes darted around the living room. For once, there weren't boxes of yarn and beads piled up on their tiny dining room table. The house was spotless and festively decorated for Halloween, and her mother was already dressed for the day.

"I got a job," her mother said, offering a weak smile. "It's only part time, but it's at Jo-Anne's. I'll be leading their weekly arts and crafts station."

Tabby's jaw dropped open as she placed her half-eaten plate on the coffee table.

"Mom! That's great," she said, rising to her feet. She wrapped her mother in a hug and sighed.

"I need to go down there today and sign a few papers," Lucinda said. "We'll catch up later, okay?"

Tabby nodded and wiped at her eyes. "I should get in the shower anyway. Thanks for my birthday breakfast."

"You're welcome. I'm going to tell your uncle to give you back your money. My roof can wait."

"Mom, really," Tabby urged. "I want to help out."

"Then you need to start by helping yourself," her mother said, giving her shoulders a light squeeze. "Maybe we can go car shopping together some time next week?"

Tabby smiled. "I'd like that."

"I'm going to take the bus into town," she said. "I love you kiddo."

"Love you too."

Lucinda slung her purse over her shoulder and headed out the door as Tabby cleared the dishes of her birthday breakfast. As she rinsed their dishes, Tabby stared out the window into the empty driveway where Donnie had dropped her off the night before and scolded herself again. She was thirty-three. She had come home to change her life and turn things around for the better. So far, she wasn't doing a very good job of making anything better at all.

Chapter Fourteen

Donnie held his breath and stared at his phone screen as the thought bubbles pulsed on his unanswered text message. It was Halloween morning, and usually Donnie busied himself by either decorating his uncle's house, watching scary movies, or working the Haunted Hike if the holiday fell on a weekend. But it was a Monday, and the only thing that Donnie had on his schedule for that particular day was to find out what he could have possibly done wrong to drive Tabby away. His text read:

Is it okay if I come over around one?

He examined the keys to her mom's car as the pulsing text bubbles continued to torture him. After what felt like an eternity, his phone dinged in reply.

Sure.

Donnie frowned. Even though things were still fairly new between him and Tabby, he could tell that something was wrong. This sort of curt, emotionless response was out of the ordinary. Normally, Tabby would have already texted him a half dozen times by now with Halloween-themed emoji-laden messages.

Was it the mustache? He wondered to himself as he stared at his reflection in the mirror. *Is she mad about the Franken-punch?*

Donnie could't wrap his mind around it. Still, it was Halloween. His *favorite* holiday, and he was on his way to see his *favorite* person. Dressed in his best pair of jeans, a band tee and a plaid flannel, Donnie readied himself to do whatever it took to figure out what was going on with Tabby. He slid behind the wheel of her mother's car, determined to not sit back this time and let silence pass between them. He had sat back too many times before and let a lack of communication ruin things between him and people he cared about. He wasn't about to let that happen again. But first, he had a very special stop to make to pick up a very special birthday/Halloween present for someone he was certain he loved.

Chapter Fifteen

Tabby hung up her wrinkled Elvira dress and stood back to admire it as she mulled over her wardrobe options for the day. All of her worldly possessions had been reduced to two large suitcases after she and her uncle removed everything out of her old room. For the time being, she was living on a couch with little to call her own and few prospects for the future. It wasn't an ideal way to start her thirty-third birthday.

With her hair still slightly damp from the shower, Tabby slipped into a pair of jeans, a tank top and a long-sleeved plaid flannel. Even though it wasn't cool enough out for long sleeves, Tabby refused to let the Florida weather discourage her fall spirit. She burned spicy pumpkin scented candles and played Halloween cartoon classics in the background as she readied herself for the day all in an attempt to evoke a festive mood.

Happy Birthday!

Tabby smiled as a text from Evan paired with a GIF of a dancing pumpkin-head man dinged on her phone. She spent the rest of the morning fielding texts, social media messages and other birthday wishes and phone calls. With each notification, her spirits grew. Still, there was one person that she wanted to see on her birthday more than anyone else. Someone she was ashamed to see.

Around 1 p.m., the crunching of tires on gravel signaled that it was time for Tabby to face the music. She steeled herself and peered out the window to see Donnie stepping out of her mother's car into the warm autumnal afternoon sunlight. Her heart almost broke to see him looking even more handsome somehow. Another stab of guilt pierced her heart as he approached the front door carrying something big, round and orange.

"Happy birthday," he said as she opened the door. In his arms was an enormous pumpkin that must have weighed thirty pounds or more.

On his face was a smile that was soft and warm, as though the events from the night before never happened.

"A pumpkin?" she said, accepting the heavy gourd. She muttered a slight "oof" sound under her breath as she carried her gift to the kitchen table. "No one's ever given me a birthday pumpkin before."

"Really?" he asked, his eyebrows furrowed. "I would think that's the most obvious gift for you in the world."

"I love it," she said, staring up at him. "Thanks for bringing back my mom's car."

"No problem," he said, the corners of his mouth turning up in a curious grin. His eyes roamed over her shoulders, down her arm and all the way to her feet.

"What?" she said, looking at her t-shirt for stains.

"We're wearing practically the same thing," he said. "That's funny, right?"

"Yeah," she said, her eyes darting between their twin wardrobes. "Spooky."

"Oh, here," he said, handing over her mother's car keys. "I hope it's not weird that I called the house this morning. You put the number down on the audition form for the Haunted Hike."

"It's fine," she reassured him.

"Anyway," he said, scratching the back of his head. "I just wanted to see if... if you're okay?"

Tabby nodded. "Yeah. I'm feeling much better," she said. "That's the last time I have punch at a party though."

"Right?" he laughed, casting his eyes to the floor. "I think what I really meant, though, was, are you *okay*?" Donnie raised his eyes and met her gaze, his expression calm and even. Tabby swallowed and braced herself for what was sure to be an awkward exchange.

She shook her head. "Not really," she said.

Donnie's lips set into a half frown and he nodded. "Can I come in?"

Tabby regarded the humble living room, with its shabby carpet and the same couch that her mom had for twenty years. Donnie couldn't possibly be comfortable in her living room that was the size of one of his waterfront mansion bathrooms. She let out a deep sigh.

"Sure."

Tabby set the pumpkin on the coffee table and shoved her pillow aside as Donnie followed her into the room. His massive frame filled the entire entryway, his head nearly touching the low ceiling. Tabby sunk down into the couch and stared at the orange pumpkin as Donnie made himself comfortable next to her. After a brief moment of shared silence and another deep sigh, Tabby started.

"I didn't want you to see where I lived," she said. "I never brought friends here growing up. I think you can guess why."

Donnie propped his elbows on his knees, his hands steepled together in thought. "Is that all?"

"No," she said.

"It's okay," he said. "I can take it."

"I don't think I can go back to school," she admitted. "I crunched the numbers and I won't be able to afford it. Not now, anyway. Maybe never."

Donnie scoffed and hung his head. Tabby's face flamed as he let out a low chuckle.

"So that's it then? You're just embarrassed about your house and school?"

Tabby clenched her jaw as he shook his head and smiled at her.

"Yes!"

Donnie reached over and grabbed her hand as a fat, hot tear rolled down her cheek. "I don't care about any of that," he said. "I told you, you can talk to me."

Tabby wiped at her face and sniffed as he gave her a reassuring squeeze.

"I thought I did something wrong," he said. "I know I don't always express myself so well either, but I don't want that to happen with us."

"I didn't know if you would understand," she shrugged.

"I have my own baggage too," he said. "I'm a grown man still living with my uncle. I'm lost when it comes to running my business. You don't judge me on that."

"I suppose," she said, wiping at her face again. "It's just that I've been hiding and running away from this part of myself for a long time."

Donnie shook his head. "You don't have to hide with me."

Tabby sniffed again and gave him a half smile. "You wanna help me carve this pumpkin?"

Donnie grinned back at her and his new mustache twitched. She laughed despite herself and squeezed his hand.

"Heck yeah I do," he said.

"Good," she said. "I'll go get a knife."

***

The warm glow of an illuminated jack-o'-lantern shone its toothy grin from atop the TV console later that evening. Jamie Lee Curtis cowered in a closet on the screen and let out a shriek of terror. Tabby clutched Donnie's arm and huddled under the blanket as a bowl of fresh popcorn warmed her lap. She jumped as the killer slashed at the metal clothes hangers and buried her face in Donnie's arm.

"I thought you said that you've seen this a million times?" he laughed, placing a kiss on top of her head.

"Yeah, but it still gets me," she said.

"We could still go out if you want," he said. "This is almost over."

"Nah," she said. "We still have to watch *Pumpkinhead.*"

"Now you're talking," he said, reaching for a handful of popcorn.

"This is the best birthday I've had in a long time," she admitted, staring back up at him in the light of the flickering television. "Thank you."

Donnie leaned down and planted a salty kiss on her lips, and she was whisked back to their first date only a few days before. It was almost as though they were getting to know each other all over again, cocooned in their own little nest and illuminated by the soft glow of a horror movie. Tabby's Halloween birthday wish had come true.

"You know," he said with a grin, his eyebrows wagging suggestively. "Uncle Ty is still in Las Vegas."

"Oh yeah?" she said.

"*And* I still have a working VHS player in my room."

Tabby pursed her lips together in a wry grin. "I suppose I could get one more use out of my Elvira costume," she said, crunching on a piece of popcorn. "But you have to wear your baseball uniform again."

Donnie's smile spread even wider. "I'll call us a cab."

Tabby bit her lower lip and grinned as she settled in next to Donnie until the credits rolled on the greatest Halloween movie of all time. What she said was true; she wasn't out on the town with friends or exploring some new, far flung town. She wasn't in her own apartment yet, and hadn't met any of the goals she had set out for herself when she moved back to town. But she had found something unexpected and new and sweet in Donnie Treadwell. Despite everything else that was uncertain and unsettled in her life, she had a new friend and more in Donnie.

As they rode back together toward Donnie's home that night, they were followed by the light of a full Halloween moon. Tabby gazed up and made one final birthday wish upon it. She closed her eyes, squeezed Donnie's hand and hoped that it would come true.

Chapter Sixteen

"Where should I store these tombstones?"

Donnie stood back as he released a flood of water out into the woods. It gushed through the trees in a loud whoosh and his haunted lagoon was no more. In the distance, Tabby held up a styrofoam board that read "HERE LIES FRED, TOO BAD HE'S DEAD."

"Take them to Melissa up at the shed," he shouted. "She'll show you where they go!"

"Thanks!" she called back.

Donnie smiled as Tabby stalked down the path wheeling a palette of decorations behind her. It was November first, the traditional Haunted Hike clean-up day, and he and his crew were busy tucking away all of his sets and scary props until next year. After all of the plastic skulls, fog machines and exterior illumination accessories were safely stored, Donnie would be able to crunch his final numbers and see his profits from the Halloween attraction that year. So far, he was already up by more than thirty percent in ticket sales alone, and closing weekend proved to be the busiest event ever. By all accounts, it looked like Donnie was going to be able to resurrect the Haunted Hike for at least one more year.

Tabby returned as he was breaking down the drive-in theater props with two glasses of iced tea at hand. The magic of Halloween had disappeared overnight and with it the unseasonably cool weather. It was hot again and he was grateful for the refreshing drink and even more refreshing company.

"Melissa said she and Stef are almost finished breaking down the back end of the trail," she said, taking a gulp of her tea. "It's sad to see it all put away."

"Yeah, cleanup is always the hard part," he said, wiping a bead of sweat from his brown. "Thanks for coming out to help today."

"Glad to," she said. "I'll be back at the café in the morning, and then I have to hit the job boards again."

Donnie pursed his lips, unable to decide whether or not he should say what was on his mind. What had *been* on his mind, for that matter. He had been waiting for weeks now to bring up the topic of hiring Tabby permanently, but never could seem to find the right words or the right time.

"You know," she said, her gaze set up in the trees. "It would be easy to string this entire path with twinkle lights."

"Oh?" he said, leaning up against one of the rusted out cars. "Go on."

Tabby eyed the rusty old cars where her drive-in post had been. "You could show classic holiday movies here," she said, turning to the area where the graveyard used to be. "Over there you can set up a sleigh with some reindeer and some artificial trees."

"I like where this is going," Donnie nodded.

"And then at the end, instead of a chainsaw killer, you can have Santa!"

Donnie smiled and ran his thumb and his forefinger along his jaw in thought. "Are you suggesting that Ty Treadwell's should have a Holiday Hike?"

"Exactly," she said, propping a hand on her hip.

"We would probably have to start planning for that right away," he mused. "I don't know anything about decorating for Christmas though."

"That's okay," she said. "It was just an idea."

"Here's an idea," he said. "Come work for me."

Tabby furrowed her brow and shifted on her heels. "What do you mean?"

"I *mean*," he said, putting down his empty glass. "I need you to help me run the Holiday Hike. I want to do it."

"But I don't know anything about organizing an event like that," she said. "I'm not qualified."

"I think you're plenty qualified," Donnie said. "Plus, it was your idea. You're smart, and I know you're a hard worker. Why wouldn't you be able to do it?"

"I don't know," she said, holding her hands to her cheeks. "Is that a good idea though? Us working together again?"

"Won't know until we try," he said.

"What if it goes bad?" she said, snaking her arms around his waist. "What if I screw up? Or what if we have a huge fight halfway through the season?"

Tabby leaned into him as he placed a kiss on her sweaty forehead.

"Then we figure it out," he said. "You need a job, and I need your creative vision. Let's do it."

Tabby sighed into his chest as he stared out into the property surrounding his Family Fun Park. *His* Family Fun Park. Eventually, he would get used to thinking of it that way. Maybe Uncle Ty wouldn't have been daring enough to try something new like a Holiday Hike, but it was up to Donnie now to make this thing work. He might not have total faith in himself, but he had faith in Tabby. He had faith in *them*.

"Well, then, I accept," she said, sealing their deal with a slow, sweet kiss. "On one condition."

"What's that?" he asked, stroking the back of her hair.

Tabby smiled back up at him. Her eyes shone with a playful glimmer that he had come to love. "You have to play Santa."

Donnie rolled his eyes. "Fine," he said. "Can I be a scary Santa?"

"*No*," she said, rolling his eyes at him in return. "It's settled then. I'll come help you make the Holiday Hike at Ty Treadwell's a thing, and you'll trade in your swamp creature suit for a Santa suit."

"Well, not so fast," he said. "I have a condition too."

Tabby pursed her lips and wiggled her eyebrows. "Want me to be one of Santa's helpers?"

"No, but that's really tempting," he said, the image of her dressed in a skimpy elf costume nearly wrecking his train of thought. "My condition is that when you're ready, you should sign up for college."

"I want to," she said, crossing her arms. "It seems impossible, though. I can't afford it."

"You can't afford not to," he said. "Even if it's just one class, I think you should try. Otherwise, you'll never know."

She sighed and raised her eyes to the sky in thought. "You're right. I shouldn't give up so easily."

"So, we have a deal then?" Donnie said.

Tabby nodded and tugged at his arm. "Come on. We have more cleanup to do."

Donnie tugged back and pulled her to him again. Tabby leaned into him as he tucked a strand of pale pink hair behind her ear.

"Tabby," he said, his eyes searching hers. Her lips curled into a smile.

"What?"

"Thank you," he said.

"For what?"

"For helping me," he said. "For always encouraging me."

"That's what you do when you care about someone." She placed a hand along the fresh scruff of his cheek as Donnie closed his eyes. He held her hand to his face and sighed.

"I love you," he said. "I think I have for a while. I just didn't know when was the right time to —"

Tabby leaned in and muffled his words with a frenzied flurry of kisses. Her lips tasted of sweet tea and salt, perfectly complex and delicious all at once, just like her. He pressed her hand to his heart and only opened his eyes when they finally came up for air. She was still there, her body molded against his and smiling.

"I love you back."

They stayed there, wrapped in each other's arms on the very trail they had both traveled so many times before. Even though time had passed and changed them both, in the end, they were still two Halloween crazy kids in love and in the very place they were always meant to be.

"Hey, you two love birds! We still have a bunch of cobwebs to clean up!"

Donnie spun his head around to see Melissa, sweaty and covered in glitter and cottony faux webbing. Tabby laughed and waved to her at the entrance of the trail.

"Guess it's time to get back to work," she said, giving him one last peck on the lips for good measure.

"Hey, Melissa!" Donnie called out, giving Tabby a wink. "We've got something to tell you!"

Epilogue

Three years later...

"Where do you want these rubber bats to go?"

Tabby looked up from her checklist at her mother as she held up a dozen realistic-looking black bats strung on invisible fishing lines. Lucinda was wearing one of her newest creations, an orange t-shirt with jack-o'-lantern iron-on decals. Tabby was still getting used to the idea of her mother also being her employee, but overall, working alongside her mom was actually pretty nice.

"Those are going to the cemetery," she said. "I think there's a step ladder there that you can use to hang them up."

"Oh, and I got you some more black tulle from Jo-Anne's too," she said. "It's in the back of my car."

"Perfect," she said, checking off a box on her list. "Thanks, Mom."

"You got it, sweetie," Lucinda said. She plodded down the path toward the cemetery as the bat decorations bounced comically along with her. Tabby grinned to herself, happy to see her mother out in the world and lending them a hand.

"Oof!"

Tabby lurched forward as something small and powerful attacked her in a frenzy from behind. A pair of small hands wrapped around the back of her leg and squeezed as a little body attached itself to her. She whipped around to see a pair of dark eyes sparkling up at her.

"Aunt Tabby!"

"Cody!"

Tabby squealed and scooped up the squirmy two-year-old. He was the spitting image of his Uncle Donnie in denim overalls.

"Where did you come from?" she asked.

Cody pointed a chubby finger toward the parking lot as Melissa and a heavily pregnant Stef rounded the corner.

"That kid never stops running!" Melissa huffed.

"Hi! I thought you guys weren't coming until the Holiday Hike," Tabby said, her mouth open wide.

"We wanted to surprise you," Stef said, giving Melissa a side-eye. "Donnie said there was a new attraction at the Haunted Hike this year that we *had* to see."

"I know," Tabby said, shaking her head. "He's been talking about it all week. He's been so secretive."

"How's school going?" Melissa asked, scooping Cody from Tabby's arms.

"Not bad. I should be getting my AA in the spring if everything goes well." Tabby nodded. "How are things at the farm?"

Melissa shook her head and gave Stef a side-eye. "Well, the barn needs a new set of doors and Stef keeps bringing home a new animal every time I look the other way."

"Stop," Stef said. "You love it."

"I know," Melissa said. "So where's Donnie at?"

"He's on the trail somewhere working on the sets." Tabby nodded. Her back pocket vibrated as she reached for her phone.

"Speak of the devil," she said, scanning her text messages. "He says to meet him in the cemetery?"

"Well, let's go then," Melissa said, setting her son down on the trail.

With her clipboard in hand, Tabby ventured down the half-decorated path toward the Haunted Hike cemetery. It was early September, and due to popular demand, Ty Treadwell's would be opening their famous attraction a full week earlier than usual that year. She and Donnie had to hire twice as many actors and support crew than they normally did for the event, which drew in crowds from Naples all the way to Sarasota.

"So, Donnie said you two put in an offer on a place?" Melissa asked as they passed the haunted lagoon.

"We did," Tabby nodded. "It's just down the road from my mom's house. It still feels strange to think that I'm going to be a homeowner."

"You two deserve it," Stef said. "You've really turned things around here."

"Thanks," Tabby said. "I've grown really attached to this place."

The group passed the drive-in theater set and descended upon the cemetery where Lucinda was hard at work hanging bats. The traditional tombstones had already been set out and covered with leaf litter, Spanish moss, and piles of styrofoam bones. However, there appeared to be a new tombstone in the center of it all that was unusual and out of place.

"Oh good!" her mom said, stepping down from the ladder. "You're just in time. There's something you need to see."

Tabby frowned and cocked her head to the side as she passed through the cemetery gates toward the odd-looking new graveyard addition. The tombstone was obviously different from the rest, and instead of skulls or black cats, this one was decorated in hearts with the words "WILL U B MINE?"

"Is this supposed to be for the Valentine's Hike?" Tabby asked, pointing to the out-of-place décor.

The mound of leaves at the foot of the tombstone shook and quaked as a ghastly voice moaned from beneath the ground. A pair of gnarled, decaying hands shot out from the earth, reaching toward her. Tabby screamed and held out her hands in self-defense as a figure rose and belted out a deep, booming laugh.

"Donnie Treadwell!" Tabby yelled. "You scared me half to death!"

Donnie continued to laugh as he smiled up at her through his zombie disguise. He brushed the leaves from his beard and tattered shirt and shook them from his head.

"That was the effect I was hoping for," he said. "Sorry babe, it was too good to resist."

"I know. You can't help it," Tabby said, looking over her shoulder. "Hey did you know that Melissa and Stef are here?"

Tabby looked back down to see that Donnie had risen from his leaf-covered grave. He was crouched at her feet with one knee extended and held out a very small pumpkin in the palm of his hand. A zap of lightning shot up her spine as she turned to see Melissa, Stef and her mother huddled together at the edge of the cemetery. Melissa's zoom lens camera had somehow magically appeared around her neck. She waved and snapped their picture as an undead hand slipped into hers.

"Donnie, it isn't my birthday yet," she said. "What's all this about?"

Tabby's voice was shaky as she looked back down at him. Part of her suspected what his zombie trap was about, but she almost couldn't allow herself to believe it. A cut had been made all around the top of the carved mini pumpkin that he was still holding in his hand, and the prospect of what might be inside both terrified and thrilled her all at once.

"I know," he said, his eyes flicking down to the tiny jack-o-lantern. "Open it."

Tabby bit her lower lip and tried to remember to breathe as she grasped the stem of the pumpkin and lifted the lid. Nestled inside the hollowed out little pumpkin shell was a velvet pillow box and a perfect pink tourmaline ring. Tabby blinked and pressed a hand to her lips.

"So?" Donnie said, clearing his throat. "Wanna get married?"

Tabby laughed as Donnie gazed up at her, his zombie makeup already sweating off into his beard. She plucked the ring out from its unusual packaging and slid it on her finger. It was just the right size.

"Heck yeah, I do."

Tabby wrapped her arms around his neck as a series of wolf whistles, applause and shutter snaps sounded in the distance. She kissed him, green zombie makeup and all, and they fell together in the pile of leaves as friends and family watched on. Donnie hugged her back and breathed a sigh of relief into the crook of her neck.

"I was scared you might not say yes," he said, as she cradled his face in her hands.

"No way," she said. "You can't get rid of me."

"'Til death do us part, then?" he chuckled.

Tabby shook her head. "Nuh uh. I'm not letting you off that easy," she said. "I want the afterlife too."

"Fine," he said. "I bet you'd make a sexy ghost."

"Ew!" Melissa said, snapping another picture. "You two are so macabre!"

Tabby and Donnie laughed and because they knew it was true. In a million years, Tabby would have never believed she would want to hold down a steady job, buy a house or even get married. Donnie and his dark sense of humor and sweet sensibilities changed all that in her.

"See, that's what I love about you," he said, wrapping her arms around her waist. "You're just as twisted as me."

"'Spooky' is the preferred term, thank you," she said, going in for one last kiss. "It's what I love about you too."

After another long, leafy kiss, Tabby helped him to his feet, all too aware of the weight of her new piece of jewelry on her hand. She proudly showed her ring off to her mother and soon-to-be sisters-in-law as Donnie made zombie noises and stumbled after Cody through the cemetery.

"So, let me know when you're ready to plan the wedding," her mom said, admiring the sparkling pink stone. "I can get you a great discount on invitations and decorations, of course."

"Nah, we won't need any of that stuff," Donnie said, scooping Tabby up from behind. "We can just elope in Transylvania."

"Ooh, or maybe we can find a real haunted house to get married at!" Tabby said, her eyes growing wide as she met Donnie's gaze. "Or we could just have a —"

"Halloween wedding?" he said, completing her sentence.

"Exactly."

"I'm starving," Donnie said. "I've got a reservation for everyone down at The Edison. Pizza burgers on me!"

"Yes!" Cody squealed and zoomed down the path as Melissa and Stef followed at his heels.

Tabby smiled as she and Donnie walked hand-in-hand back toward the parking lot, trailing their family. A hot breeze rustled the leaves overhead as a hint of fall-scented air kissed her cheeks. She was a much different person now than the wild, carefree nomad she used to be, but she liked the shape her new life was taking. Donnie kissed the top of her hand as they left their Haunted Hike for the night, knowing full well that it would be waiting for them again the next day and all the other days after it. For now, Tabby's heart was full of family, Halloween and a love that was spooky, sweet, and uniquely theirs.

About the Author

Wendy Dalrymple is a professional copywriter living in sunny Tampa Bay, FL. When she's not writing, you can find her camping with her family, painting bad wall art, trying to grow pineapples, learning 90s radio hits to play on her ukulele, or walking her dog. She is the author of over two dozen romance novels and novellas available exclusively at Scribd.com. Keep up with Wendy at www.wendydalrymple.com[1]!

1. http://www.wendydalrymple.com

Also by Wendy Dalrymple

Miss Claus and the Millionaire
Chasin' Jason
Kissing Christmas Goodbye
Tamsen's Hollow
Two Friends and a Funeral
Spring Fling
Here You Come Again
Two Scoops
White Ibis
Love in the Dark
Kiss My Grits
I Love You S'more
The Ghost and Mr. Moore
My Halloween Romance
Roser Park

Watch for more at https://www.wendydalrymple.com.

About the Author

Wendy Dalrymple writes cozy, low-heat romances inspired by everyday people. When she's not writing happily-ever-afters, you can find her camping with her family or walking her dog. Wendy Dalrymple writes cozy, low-heat romances inspired by everyday people. When she's not writing happily-ever-afters, you can find her camping with her family or walking her dog.

Read more at https://www.wendydalrymple.com.

Ingram Content Group UK Ltd.
Milton Keynes UK
UKHW040707070323
418105UK00020B/241